# Chasing the Wind

Other books by
*ABIE ALEXANDER*

*AN AMERICAN IN SEARCH OF GOD*
*SOMETIMES WHEN WE MEET*
*MEMORIES AND MIRAGES*
*FOR THE LOVE OF ARMINE*
*THE MIGRANT AND THE MAVERICK*
*OF MINGLED YARN*

# Chasing the Wind

### Abie Alexander

AA
BOOKS

Copyright © 2008 Abie Alexander

First published 2008  Infinity Publishing, PA, USA

**AA Books** ISBNs

| | |
|---|---|
| *Print* | 978-1-946593-39-9 |
| *EPUB* | 978-1-946593-04-7 |
| *AZW3* | 978-1-946593-05-4 |
| *MOBI* | 978-1-946593-06-1 |
| *PDF* | 978-1-946593-07-8 |

Published in the United States of America

Cover illustration: Cheryl Smith

AA
BOOKS

7919 Mandan Road #103
Greenbelt, Maryland. USA 20770-2828
+1 (301) 335-5632
aa-books@outlook.com
www.abiealexander.com

*For*

*Barbie*

*&*

*Camilla, Robert, Ramona,*
*Remington, Martin, and*
*their mother Sara*

## *A Note to the Reader*

Like many other societies around the world that customarily add honorific extensions to names, the Somi tribe described in this book prefixes the names of males with *'Sau'* and that of females with *'Nau'* when addressing or referring to another person of their own tribe (but not to the names of aliens outside of their tribe). Likewise, the Somis address elders of their own tribe by a respectful generic term (e.g. *'Aga'* for elder brother). As these customs are indicative of the social mores of the tribe these have been preserved in the story, to the extent possible, without making them an impediment to reading. The tenor of conversations in the Somi tongue has been attempted to be preserved not by a literal word-for-word translation, but by using the nearest colloquial equivalent in the English language.

*"If thou seest the oppression of the poor, and violent perverting of judgment and justice in a province, marvel not at the matter ..."*

Ecclesiastes 5:8

# Contents

## Chapter 1

In the backyard of their house, that mid-afternoon, the mother foresaw her son's death.

She watched dumbfounded, from nearly thirty feet away, a gray miasma cover Jacob's face, even as he strode purposefully – as he always did – towards the house. Sensing a sinister omen, fear drained her strength in an instant and she slowly sank down with her head in her hands.

"Ma, are you alright?" Jacob asked as he ran towards her and kneeling put his arm around her shoulders.

"It is nothing, son," she replied not looking up. "I may have stood up rather suddenly."

"Why don't you go in and lie down?" suggested Jacob. "I will hang the clothes up to dry."

"No, son, I will be alright. You go on inside. This is not difficult work. I only need to hang them up. Moreover, I need some fresh air. I will finish this quickly and then come and make tea for you."

"OK, but please be careful. You work too hard," Jacob said slowly standing up.

"I will be fine. Don't worry about me," she said wiping her forehead with the threadbare cotton apron that was knotted over her left shoulder. "I nearly forgot, Rosie is in the house waiting for you," she called after him raising her voice a notch.

Inwardly she prayed, "Oh, Lord, don't take my son's life. Please do not let him die." She had seen her son change noticeably in the last six months, breaking off his engagement to his childhood sweetheart Rosie and then abandoning his clockwork daily schedule for an uncharacteristically haphazard routine that seemed to have no rhyme or reason. She did not even know what he did for a living anymore. What concerned her most was his gradual falling away from the church. Gone were the excited preparations for Sunday School and the Christian Endeavor youth group. Now there were times he even skipped the Sunday service, something unthinkable just a few months earlier.

"May the Lord have mercy on me," she murmured as she bent down to pick up another piece of clothing from the aluminum basin at her feet.

When Jacob stepped into the kitchen he found Rosie sitting on a low bamboo stool tending the smoky wood fire over which rested a shiny aluminum kettle. She turned around to look up and, as always, he was struck by her arresting beauty. From this angle, crouched down low, she looked even smaller and more delicate than she was. With her head cocked up towards him, the small birthmark on her right jaw stood out in sharp contrast to the smooth skin. The full lips and the dark eyes did not diminish her childlike, almost angelic, appearance.

But Jacob well knew that this was deceptive. Rosie was more tenacious than a terrier and totally fearless when it came to fighting for what she thought was right. She was always the ardent defender of the underdog. An *amicus curiae*, if you will, of the court of public opinion, who believed in never giving up the fight against the rich and powerful who trampled on the poor like chaff.

"Hello! Been here long?" was all he could manage.

"Hi! No, I just came. Thought I'd make some tea while waiting for you to show up. Where have you been?"

"Nowhere in particular."

"Come on, you can tell me. We are in this together, remember?" she teased him.

"No, I don't mean to hide anything from you. Have you heard the news?

"Which one?"

"Our Chief Minister Sau Davidson Chapang has sold our forestland to the alien Warbaris," said Jacob.

"He did what?" Rosie cried plaintively, rising from the stool and facing him with arms akimbo, anger writ large on her beautiful face. "No, he cannot do that! He may be the Chief Minister but he has no powers to sell community land! That too, our sacred forest! The forest is ours!" Rosie, livid with anger, almost shouted.

"I know. But we are a passive people. We make kings out of the ones we elect and we turn ourselves into slaves. Sau Chapang did it. He sold the forest. I know this for a fact," said Jacob.

"Who told you? If this is true, we need to do something to stop the sale."

"There is probably very little we can do. I'm becoming more of a pessimist or a fatalist with each passing day," he said ruefully.

"I won't let this happen! Sau Chapang is a monster!" spat out Rosie in disgust.

"I completely agree. What bugs me is that Sau Chapang knows he is doing wrong. He knows his corruption is not a secret. Everyone knows it. Yet he doesn't care. He is literally thumbing his nose at us."

"I know. There must be something that we can do. We need to act quickly," said Rosie desperately.

"I don't know what we can do. I'm not good at law. I was told he has found a loophole somewhere. What he is doing is transferring the ninety-nine-year-old British lease that is expiring next month to Durgeshwar, the slimiest of all Warbaris, for another ninety-nine years. No tenders, no public announcements. Just a shady, secret deal at the Evening Club."

"Sometimes I think the EC is the seat of power. All the wheeling and dealing takes place at that Club. How much did he get out of this, Jacob?" asked Rosie, her anger rising again.

"You won't believe the figure. It's the biggest moolah he has ever got in a single deal." Jacob paused dramatically. "Eight digits! Ten million *katas* in our currency! Can you believe that? It is more than the aid given to the eastern province after the typhoon three months ago."

"What will he do with all that money? How much wealth does a human being need anyway?" asked Rosie rhetorically.

"It was paid to him in cash this morning. I believe it came to over two hundred thousand American dollars. Durgeshwar starts the fencing tomorrow. I can bet in less than three months' time all the old oak and teak trees will be chopped down and carted off outside our province. I knew when the crafty Durgeshwar offered to set up an eye clinic on the edge of the forest he was planning something sinister. The gullible public thought he was being philanthropic. It was the camel getting one foot in the tent."

"I remember that well. But you hated Sau Chapang from the beginning," said Rosie.

"Yes, that's true. It happened when I was in school and Sau Chapang was just starting out in politics. He was only a minor elected representative then. This happened at a function honoring the disabled and he was the chief guest. When he had to present a young disabled girl with a memento, he waited at the podium for her to drag herself from the back of the room instead of going up to her and giving it himself. I was disgusted," said Jacob making a face. "It betrayed his callousness and insensitivity."

"I can't believe he did that."

"Oh yes, he did. And all his actions since then have confirmed my fears. He is utterly selfish and corrupt. Now he has sold our birthright and our heritage," said Jacob bitterly.

"This is a tragedy. What about the others in the cabinet?" asked Rosie.

"They have all been bought off – mostly through blackmail. Sau Chapang has videotapes of most of the old lechers in flagrante delicto in Bangkok or Dubai. They did not realize what they were getting into when he generously let them use his secretly owned apartments in those places."

"And the two holy, holy ones?" asked Rosie.

"Them?" laughed Jacob contemptuously. "He has made one the Chairman of the Planning Commission and the other the Chairman of the Reforms Commission. Both are toothless institutions that are nothing but a drain on the exchequer. But it suits them well. They can be Lord Pooh-Bah in public and revered elder at church, while openly milking the state coffer."

Rosie looked at him wordlessly for a minute and quietly sat down. The tea had nearly boiled dry and she added more water.

Just then Jacob's mother came in carrying the large aluminum basin and the plastic buckets.

"Ma, why didn't you call me?" asked Rosie jumping up to help.

Jacob walked away to his room and flopped down on his back. It was all getting very complicated. He knew he was too far in to get out now.

"Patriotism may indeed be the last resort of scoundrels," he said to himself. "And fittingly it has no exit strategy."

His reveries were interrupted by Rosie calling from the kitchen, "Come, have tea. It is ready!"

"Coming!" called out Jacob, getting off the bed.

Rosie could conjure up a delicious cup of tea, Jacob knew, and sure enough, there were three cups of milk tea set on saucers on the low center table and a plate of buttered white bread in the middle. Jacob joined Ma and Rosie at the table, pulling up a bamboo stool from the corner and said a perfunctory grace before savoring the aroma of freshly brewed tea. Ma held out the plate of bread first to Rosie and then to Jacob before taking a slice for herself. They sipped their tea in silence, lost in their own thoughts.

"Do you want some rice, son?" asked Ma.

"No, Ma. Bread will do fine. I had something to eat when I was in town. What about you, Rosie?"

"No, I am not hungry either. Thanks."

When tea was done, Rosie carried the cups and saucers to the dishwashing area in the corner of the kitchen. She poured water into an aluminum basin from a brass jar by the wall, rolled up her jeans to calf level so they wouldn't get wet, and squatted on her haunches. Ma meanwhile opened the wire-mesh door of the small wooden cabinet by the fireplace to keep the plate of leftover bread inside. Jacob picked up the wooden bowl with the *kuwa* (areca nut and betel leaf) and started paring an areca nut with the folding knife. The cups washed, Rosie joined Ma and Jacob near the fireplace unrolling and smoothing down her jeans as she sat on the low bamboo stool. Ma began preparations for the evening meal by taking out potatoes and onions and other vegetables from the bottom shelf of the cabinet and laying them all out on the bamboo tray.

"I must be going," Rosie said.

"How is Nau Elsie?" asked Ma.

"Thank you, Ma is a lot better now. She will go back to work from next week. Thank you, Ma!" replied Rosie.

Jacob walked her to the road. When they were clear of the house, Rosie surreptitiously glanced around them to be sure no one was nearby and then whispered looking straight ahead, "Move out of Chiang and Minglai immediately."

"What?" asked Jacob surprised.

"You heard me. Break up the Minglai camp and move north," she hissed looking straight ahead.

"Okay! Got you. Noted. They have already left Chiang and are moving north to Minglai. I will pass the word. They will move elsewhere instead. How did you get this information, may I ask?'

"A little bird told me," she replied smiling.

"The standard answer again, huh?"

"Have I ever been wrong?" countered Rosie.

"No, I must admit you haven't. But I'm curious who your source is."

"Jacob, you haven't ever told me who your sources are and I stopped asking you that long ago. It's best we didn't know who each other's secret sources are. If the worst comes to the worst, they can never get out of us what we didn't have in the first place, now can they?" she said with a blend of hard-nosed pragmatism and romantic fatalism.

Looking at her lithe body in the hip-hugging jeans (a rebel against custom, she seldom wore the traditional *luan,* a sarong-like wraparound), Jacob said with admiration, "Beauty and brains and tough as nails! I wonder looking at you sometimes if we have done the right thing. Maybe we should elope to another country, start life afresh, raise a family and live happily ever after."

A shadow crossed Rosie's face. She seemed to hesitate between regret and hope. With a visible effort, she said, "Let's not go there. It was your decision that we break-up for the sake of the Movement. I thought we could have each other and still fight for the cause together. But you would not agree. We can never go back," she said with finality, tightening her lips and shaking her head.

Watching her right foot involuntarily tap the ground, Jacob could only say, "I thought when it's all over ..."

But Rosie cut him short decisively. "Let's not discuss this any further. It is pointless. There cannot be any going back. We have crossed the point of no return. We took the decision with our eyes wide open. That's the end of it."

Jacob knew that it was futile to argue. He remembered the intense agony he had gone through after a minor lovers' tiff soon after they had fallen in love. That seemed ages ago now. He steeled himself and said, "I don't deny the decision was mine. But it was not because I don't love you. On the contrary. You are the only one I love still. But we would have become millstones around each other's necks and shackles around our ankles when the fight got hotter."

Rosie gazed at him steadily as she said, "Let's not talk about love. My heart has hardened into granite." Then with a twinkle in her eye and a forced smile, she added, "How the mighty have fallen! A pious Sunday school teacher once – and now, a violent jingoist and anarchist."

With that she turned and walked away, waving her hand in silent goodbye.

"Are you going home?" he called after her.

"Yes, but I'm taking the long way around," she said turning around briefly.

Her gibe had cut him to the quick. "Is that what I have become? An anarchist and a jingoist? Am I only a little better than the run-of-the-mill terrorist?" he asked himself as he turned and walked slowly home.

Ma was washing the rice when he entered the kitchen.

"Edwin hasn't come home yet. What's the time?" asked Ma.

"He will come any minute now. Classes must have ended fifteen minutes ago."

"Son, are you going out again?" Ma asked with a quaver in her voice.

"I have to go, Ma. There's some work I need to get done," replied Jacob evasively, not looking up.

"Don't stay out too late. Remember what your father taught you when he was alive. It is only crooks and thieves who move around under cover of darkness."

## Chapter 2

Rosie walked briskly up the lane leading to the main road. The climb was broken by two sets of steps but that did not slow her down. She did not have to walk too far before a taxi came along. It was close to the end of the workday and the taxis were all headed out to the government offices to pick up employees going home at the end of the day. The driver did not wait for more passengers but sped towards the center of town with just her in the backseat and another man who was already in the front seat next to the driver. When they reached the main government Secretariat, she tapped the driver on the shoulder and handed him a five kata note. Stepping out, she crossed the road and strode into the imposing government building. The clerks were all leaving early, with an hour still left on the clock. "The lone salmon headed against a tide of shirkers," she thought as she walked against the flow and climbed the stairs quickly to the second floor. Rosie did not enter any of the myriad rooms to the left and right but walked swiftly down the broad hallway straight across to the rear of the building. Hastily glancing over her shoulder to see if anyone was tailing her she ran down the stairs to the ground level, weaving amongst the government employees heading for the rear exit. The crowd moving to the rear exit was much thinner than that heading for the main gate at the front.

The Secretariat building was of such mammoth proportions that it straddled the two major roads. It was easily the biggest building in town. Stepping out into the open courtyard she dodged the groups of male dawdlers and hangers-on and melted into the throng of women making a beeline for the exit. The small crowd outside the gate jostled to get into the crammed share-taxis. Rosie did not join the waiting horde but gently (and inconspicuously, she hoped) extricated herself and walked on up the road.

Coming around the bend, she saw the army jeep, not visible from the rear gate of the Secretariat, parked by the roadside with its engine idling. It was, as always, the same vehicle – the Commandant's own, shiny and spruced up, with its dark, tinted windows. The driver was the regular one as well, polite and respectful, as she opened the unlatched door and sinuously hoisted herself to the high seat in one swift motion.

"Good evening, ma'am!" the driver greeted her obsequiously.

"Good evening, Mohan!" she responded. He did not speak English or the local language. In any case, she thought it was good policy to remain a little aloof in such situations.

As the driver shifted gears and pulled away from the curb she hoped that she had not been seen.

But she had.

The boy sitting unobtrusively at the edge of the culvert ahead pulled out his cell phone to send a monosyllabic confirmation and then quietly melted away.

***

Jacob waited until it was dark. He spent the time reading Ché Guevara's Guerilla Warfare. Although he was at heart a pacifist and had abjured violence, he was fascinated by Ché's story. He always marveled at how idealism and sheer courage had transformed an asthmatic medical student into a fiery revolutionary who defeated neocolonialist forces and the lackeys of the powerful nations of the world. Ché was his superhero, the violence notwithstanding. As he thought of the future, Jacob's conscience was often troubled at rending the peace and tranquility of his society and causing the loss, perhaps forever, of the clannish innocence of his tribe. Given an option, he would have much preferred the nonviolent path of civil disobedience of Thoreau and Gandhi. But the government had dealt most cruelly with the neighboring Rema tribe. The federal air force had strafed and bombed Rema villages as if they were an enemy nation. And then came the occupation army and the subtler cultural and economic subjugation. The corrupt local leaders, puppets of the federal government, amassed unheard of wealth and the educated middle class likewise rapidly sank to its moral nadir pursuing affluence and forsaking diligent hard work. The same thing was happening now to his tribe too, though it had been spared the initial violence. Once an egalitarian, inherently socialist society, the Somi tribe was now being polarized into two disparate groups – the rich and the poor.

"No, there is no way out. There are no options," he told himself. "My kinfolk will not be stirred out of their apathy by mere words. Only a violent overthrow of the status quo would shake them out of their stupor."

Hiding the book under his pillow, Jacob quietly stepped into the kitchen. Ma was at the fireplace cooking and Edwin was repeating by rote the day's lessons. They both looked up as he entered.

"Will you eat now?" Ma asked.

"No, I think I will eat outside tonight. I may be late," replied Jacob.

"Dinner is almost ready. Just five more minutes," Ma said.

"No, Ma, I think I had better go."

"It is not good to eat out every day. Where do you get the money for this? Isn't it costly?" she asked.

Jacob avoided her questions. "I might be late, Ma. Don't stay up for me."

"Now remember what I told you. Don't stay out too long. Not a minute more than necessary."

"Yes, Ma," said Jacob and turned to go.

"Good night, Aga (Big Brother)!" said Edwin softly.

"You study well. I will bring you a chocolate. Good night, Ma! Good night, Edwin!"

With that, he was gone. The night air was cold and he buttoned the jacket and thrust his hands deep into his pockets. When he was clear of the house he took his cell phone out and dialed.

"Pick me up. The usual spot," he said and turned off the phone. He had an almost pathological fear of being snooped on or tracked and kept his cell phone use to the minimum.

He kept walking till he reached the junction. The car had not arrived but he did not have to wait long. When it came, he opened the front door and got in. It was Ben who was driving today.

"The boss is very angry today. He wants to see you right away," said Ben.

"Why, what happened?" Jacob asked.

"I don't know. It is better if I did not say anything."

"OK. Don't worry. I think I know what the boss is upset about," said Jacob thinking about the sale of the forestland by the government. But Jacob wondered if this could have disturbed him that much because he knew Philipson's priorities lay elsewhere.

A short distance down the road a Federal Reserve Police (FRP) patrol waved them to a halt.

"Curfew pass?" shouted the leader while the others surrounded the car, antique rifles on the ready.

Ben rolled down the window and held out the slightly tattered paper with the large government seal. The leader took his time looking at it, seeming to read it letter by letter and then handed it back. Before he let them go he came up and shone his torch in their faces and all around the interior of the car.

"Stupid FRPs! They are all illiterate louts," said Ben with disgust.

"You have heard the joke, right?" asked Jacob.

"No. How does it go?"

"The FRPs need to take a reading comprehension test for recruitment. Each of them is given a sheet to read. If they pass, they are rejected. They are overqualified for the job! If they fail, they are hired," said Jacob.

"Good one!" said Ben laughing.

When they reached the walled bungalow on the edge of town, a shadowy figure opened the massive iron gates and the car drove right up to the porch. Jacob always found his leader's house impressive. It was built less than a year ago, in the style of a Victorian mansion with a circular driveway and a covered porch under which visitors could disembark from their cars and enter the house directly.

"It is good thing Sau Philipson is so rich. He doesn't have to depend on the Movement for survival like the rest of us. Instead, he gives so much of his own money to the cause," Jacob would often tell his colleagues when they raised the issue of Philipson's wealth. But Jacob would also ponder privately, "Even if the money was all inherited, it was not a testimony to the socialism they preached." Just the living room where they held their meetings was larger in area than Jacob's entire house.

Philipson was pacing around the living room when Jacob entered.

"Ha! You have come!" he said in the Somi tongue when Jacob entered. Jacob felt that Philipson always treated him well. He had never once screamed in anger at him as he so often did with the others. And now, though he was obviously agitated, Philipson still managed a smile of welcome relaxing his stern features. "Take a seat," he added pointing to the vacant spot on one of the sofas that lined the room.

Jacob nodded to the other three in the room and was in the process of sitting down when Philipson dropped the bombshell.

"They killed three of our boys today."

Jacob felt the cold chill of fear in his stomach and his head spun.

"The bloodbath has begun," he said to himself with sorrow as he set himself gingerly down.

*\*\*\**

In the meantime, Rosie was at the army officers' club being entertained by Colonel Kattar and his junior officers. The colonel was obviously flaunting his virility by showing off Rosie as his prize catch. Rosie had realized this after their very first meeting three months ago, but she did not mind it at all because that was exactly where she wanted him.

"We killed thirty-five hostiles that day," the colonel was boasting to the junior commissioned officers arranged in a circle around him. They looked at him with the mandatorily required awe but were trying hard to keep their eyes off Rosie who was seated on a high barstool to Colonel Kattar's right with her legs crossed.

"We killed them all. They did not know what hit them. It was the perfect ambush. Me and the boys were hiding in the tall elephant grass. They walked straight into our trap. They didn't get the time to fire a single shot. Eight of them were unarmed girls. The men were carrying Chinese-made automatic guns."

"You killed them in cold blood, you bastard! And there were only seven in all – not thirty-five!" Rosie wanted to shout but she quietly sipped her beer feigning disinterest in the colonel's story.

Rosie was getting impatient. It was getting late and she knew the longer she stayed the riskier it became. She had to get the colonel alone.

"I'm feeling hungry," Rosie said coquettishly, touching the colonel's arm lightly.

"OK, dear. Let's go to my quarters for dinner!"

The officers stood up to salute and the colonel handed his bottle of Johnnie Walker ostentatiously to his batman to carry.

"Good night, boys!" he shouted out heartily as they left the club.

The colonel drove and Rosie sat beside him. The driver and the orderly sat in the rear of the jeep.

A typical army dinner was laid out when they got to the colonel's house, with several orderlies standing by. After dinner when they were alone the colonel took out a bottle of Johnnie Walker and held out a glass to Rosie.

"No, thanks. You know I don't drink hard liquor," said Rosie.

"How about some beer?" pressed the colonel.

"No, thanks. I don't drink beer after a meal."

She knew the colonel's ploy was to get her drunk and then seduce her but she had no intention of letting that happen ever. What she wanted was to talk about army operations.

"You are really brave to go after the underground rebels," Rosie said with simulated admiration. "Do you still lead the teams yourself?"

"Now that I am the Commandant I don't need to go on these search-and-destroy missions myself. But I decide where my teams go. And HQ sent me here because of my jungle warfare and counter-insurgency experience," he said proudly.

"Well, we wish you all success in stamping out this rebellion. This movement does not have the support of the majority," she lied.

The colonel poured himself another peg of whiskey. There wasn't enough. Rosie was surprised to see him pour some water in the bottle, swirl it around and pour it into his glass. "The colonel really loves his imported whiskey," thought Rosie.

"That is very important. The job of the army is to win the hearts and minds of the public. Only then can we win the war," the colonel pontificated.

Even as he talked he shook the water out of the empty bottle, carefully screwed the cap back on and placed the bottle gently on the table. The batman brought another bottle of whiskey and more ice. Rosie was surprised to hear the colonel order the batman to take good care of the empty scotch bottle.

"You cannot win our hearts and minds by raping our women and killing our young men," she thought but aloud she said, "I hope they surrender very soon. It will be a feather in your cap."

She knew what was coming next. "That is why I am asking for your help. If we can get good intelligence information we can capture them alive and prevent deaths," he said, cocking his head to the side.

"Oh, no! You would never do that. You would kill them like sitting ducks and then dump their dead bodies like carrion out of the back of army trucks in the town square," she said to herself.

"I will help you if you promise not to kill them," she said.

"I will tell my men not to shoot except in retaliation or self-defense," the colonel said.

"You must also not torment the innocent villagers and burn their houses for helping the underground."

"You are asking for too much. But for your sake I will agree," said Colonel Kattar impatiently.

She knew that these were empty promises as the colonel wanted more than anything else to completely annihilate the entire underground army—if that were possible. But she knew what to feed him.

"To save innocent people I will tell you what I know."

"Yes? Where are they hiding now?" The bloodthirsty colonel could not contain his excitement.

"There is a big group of thirty insurgents hiding in the jungle in Chiang south of Minglai," she said conspiratorially.

She knew that the colonel could not wait to get the information out to his troops. And she had deliberately inflated the number so that a larger contingent would be out a wild-goose chase to return empty-handed and dispirited. This was also a diversionary tactic that reduced the security forces around the capital and made it easier for underground units to conduct their forays into town.

But she had calculated wrong as far as the colonel's lust was concerned.

"Come and sit in my lap, darling" he suggested with a wink.

"It is getting late. I need to go. Some other time."

Colonel Kattar* came over and patted her behind. The stench of whiskey and body odor was overpowering.

"Any cutbacks in troops?" she asked casually as she extricated herself and moved away.

"Cutbacks? There is no possibility of that till these cowards surrender," he said resolutely. "On the other hand, HQ is sending two more companies next week."

Rosie pretended not to have heard. The jeep was waiting with the same driver. She saw a strange look in the eyes of the driver – a mixture of pity and desire, sympathy and lust. "He must think I'm the Commandant's concubine," she thought wryly. They sped through the empty curfewed streets. The Federal Reserve Police at the checkpoints set up for the night did not dare stop an army vehicle and simply waved them through.

Her mother had gone to bed already and was fast asleep when she noiselessly let herself in.

## Chapter 3

Philipson paced the room like a caged tiger.

"They killed them like animals. Only one of them was our member. Sau Sanga who was driving the car was our recruiter. The other two were just college kids he was trying to persuade to join. They hadn't even joined," he fumed.

"Why did the police shoot? What was the provocation?" asked Soma sitting closest to the west end of the room.

"Why did they shoot? Why did they shoot? You want to know why? I want to know too. There was no provocation. They were unarmed. The FRPs killed them for fun. These FRPs have no brains. They also have no hearts. They are animals. I'm not sure if Sau Sanga or the other two taunted them. They may have recognized Sau Sanga from his earlier brushes with the police. Or they may just have been taking revenge for last week," said Philipson smacking his right fist into the palm of left hand.

"My guess is that it was revenge for the killing of the two provincial policemen last week," offered Jacob.

"But these killers were FRPs, the Federal Reserve Police—not the provincial police," said Passa from the opposite corner.

"Precisely. Remember the hue and cry after the last fake encounter the government staged? If the provincial police retaliated now it would look like revenge. My theory is that the police got the FRPs to hit back on their behalf," said Jacob with clinical reasoning.

Everyone looked at Philipson who rubbed his jaw thoughtfully.

"That is quite possible. The army, FRPs and the provincial police are all in this together. Our battle is against all of them," said Philipson.

"The newsreader at the radio station called to tell me of the press release they got for the night's news," said Soma.

"What does it say?" asked Jacob.

"It says the boys were armed. They captured Kalashnikovs with Chinese markings."

"And you believe them?" scoffed Philipson. "Can't you see what they did? They planted the AK-47s and ammunition in the car after the killing."

"Most likely those came from the army's stock from the surrender of the Rema tribe," said Jacob.

"Anyway, we need to hit back. We need to teach them a lesson," said Philipson emphatically. "If we don't, we will look like cowards in the eyes of our own people."

"Why don't we call a strike?" asked Jacob.

"A strike is good. It will have to be a total strike. All government offices, schools, colleges, banks, post office, buses, taxis, and shops – all closed. We will shut this whole province down for two days," said Philipson.

"Isn't forty-eight hours too long? Remember the last time there was some sympathetic backlash for the daily laborers who lost their wages. We cannot afford to lose public support," said Jacob.

"That may be true but this time they have slaughtered our innocent children! I know the government employees treat our strikes like a paid holiday while the poor suffer. But that is one of the sacrifices we have to make," said Philipson.

"We can give them adequate notice so they can stock up on food," suggested Passa from the corner.

"Are you serious?" asked Jacob testily. "Where will they get money to do that? They live on daily wages."

Philipson intervened decisively. "I know there will be some suffering. But that cannot be helped. We all need to make sacrifices."

"I think we should kill a VIP," said Kamat who had been sitting quietly next to Jacob with his cap pulled low over his face.

"Brilliant!" exulted Philipson. "We will have a two-day strike and kill a big shot."

He stood with his arms crossed across his chest and his left hand thoughtfully rubbing the stubble on his right jaw. He looked around the room with his dark probing eyes, his bulging belly sticking out arrogantly.

"This is an excellent idea! Who should we pick as the target?"

Jacob tried to downplay the idea. He did not like violence. "VIPs are not easy targets. We must be cautious. This might boomerang on us," he said.

"I don't care. A tooth for a tooth and an eye for an eye!" said Soma from the other end.

"There is some truth in what Sau Jacob just said," conceded Philipson. "We don't want the air force bombing our villages like they did to the Rema tribe. Let us do just the strike for now. Sau Kamat, your idea is very good. I am not giving it up. We will do it when the time is ripe."

"Whatever you decide, boss," said Kamat.

"We need to discuss other things now. Sau Jacob, how is the fund drive coming?" asked Philipson turning to Jacob.

"I haven't got any big money these last two days. Mostly small donations from government employees."

"You have to be very careful," said Philipson. "I don't want any of our kids getting caught."

"Everyone is scared. We only tell them it is for the 'Movement'. They get the drift right away. I have told the collectors never to mention the Somi National Liberation Front or the SNLF."

"Are you sure their accounts are all straight?" asked Philipson.

"They wouldn't dare to steal," said Jacob categorically. "I pay them well and I also tell them they are playing with their lives if they cheat on us."

"We need to watch out also for cunning thieves who might use our name to get rich. If any of you hear anything just let me know," said Philipson wagging a finger.

"Ever since we forced the last thief to do frog jumps in front of the Secretariat and carry a sandwich board reading 'I will not steal from SNLF' for a whole day, there has been no incident. That one was funny. When the police asked him to take the board off and go home, he cried and pleaded to be allowed to stay. He told them his life was in danger if he left early."

"I remember that! OK! Here's some other news. You may already have heard. It is all over town. Our Chief Minister Sau Chapang has got a kickback of ten million from the Warbari trading community who have come here to loot us."

"He should give us one million," said Soma.

"Why one million? He should give us three million," said Passa.

"I think he should split it fifty-fifty with us and give us five million," said Kamat from under his hat.

"Aren't we all forgetting something?" asked Jacob. "Sau Chapang is selling off our community forest. Shouldn't we stop the sale itself instead of squabbling over our share of the ill-gotten money?" asked Jacob.

"Let's be practical, Sau Jacob. How long can we keep this forest? Sooner or later we will need the land for houses. It is Sau Chapang pocketing the money that is the issue – not the sale itself," said Philipson.

"With all due respect, Sau Philipson, I beg to differ. I think we will be harming our future by razing the forest. Our forefathers were wise in preserving them," said Jacob quietly.

Philipson looked at him evenly. This was the first time Jacob had publicly contradicted his opinion. But Philipson knew that Jacob was invaluable. Jacob kept the accounts and managed the funds. Philipson could not trust anyone else with the money. They would not only steal but make a complete mess of the money laundering as well. Jacob's biggest advantage was that nobody even remotely suspected him of having any links with the SNLF. He was the clean-cut, church-going nice guy.

"Look, Sau Jacob, you are an idealist. Revolution is a dirty game. We need money to buy guns. We need money to buy food for our soldiers hiding in the jungle. We need money to pay all our secret workers. We need money to pay off government clerks and the police to look the other way. Between independence and idealism what will you choose?" asked Philipson.

Everyone's eyes were on Jacob. He felt the blood rush to his face and his throat constrict. He rubbed his sweaty palms together and said, "We do not have to choose one over the other. We can have both. Our freedom and our forest heritage."

Philipson decided that it was best not to argue in public with Jacob.

So, he laughed and said, "You know Sau Jacob, you are such an idealistic hothead! But you are the educated one in our group. I will think about what you said. Right now, let us deal with the state executions, okay?"

"All right. Provided we can talk about the forest later."

"Good! Here's something you would all like to hear. Gurdas has given us fifty thousand katas. It was not easy. He did not want to give more than ten thousand at first. I had to gently remind him of how his brother was killed a year ago—right in front of his own house for refusing to pay. He paid up very quickly when I told him that," chuckled Philipson.

"The Warbaris are all chamber pots! Even a rabbit is enough to scare them out of their wits!" scoffed Soma from the west end and everyone laughed.

"Hey, Sau Ben!" called out Philipson into the next room. "Bring in the whiskey and rum and enough glasses. You all give Jacob and me a few minutes. I need to give him the money and the accounts."

Jacob got up and followed Philipson into the next room. He had been there before. It was a smaller room done up like a study with a massive teakwood table and a modern executive chair. The bookshelves on the wall were lined with hardbound editions. Jacob knew that Philipson hadn't read even one of the books. The table was spotlessly clean. There wasn't a single sheet of paper on it.

Philipson walked over behind the table and pulled out an ordinary plastic shopping bag that he held upside down and a bundle wrapped in newsprint fell out. Philipson pushed it towards Jacob and said, "Here's the money. Count it."

Jacob unwrapped the newspaper covering to reveal bundles of hundred and five hundred kata notes held together by rubber bands. He counted them quickly like a professional bank teller and wrote down the amounts.

"Forty thousand," Jacob said adding up the numbers he had jotted down on the newspaper wrapping.

"Right. I had to use ten thousand for expenses."

Jacob knew better than to ask what the expenses were. He merely nodded. Philipson had no clue about accounts and did not think the short amounts would be marked against his name. But Jacob, the diligent accountant that he was, had tagged all these against Philipson. Jacob did some quick math in his head to figure out the total. Today's shortfall would take the cumulative amount close to the six hundred thousand mark. This was a lot of money to be ignored.

"Any payments to be made?" asked Jacob.

"Send fifteen thousand to our fourth unit. Someone will come to you tomorrow."

"I will need to put this in a bank and draw from another account."

"Do that. Come, we need to get back to the jokers out there."

"OK. I have a message for you. Our unit that moved from Chiang must leave Minglai by daybreak. They need to go elsewhere."

"How reliable is the source?" asked Philipson.

'It is the same source. Never been wrong so far."

"Right. I'll take care of it. You go back to the room. I'll send a message out right now. These things can't wait. You should have told me this when you came in."

"Sorry. You were so worked up about the fake encounter."

"Why didn't you stop me? We cannot take any chances with these things. Every minute counts."

"It won't happen again. I promise." Jacob was contrite.

When he got back to the room he realized that further intelligent conversation would not be possible that night. They must have soaked up the whiskey and rum like the parched earth soaks up the first rain.

When Philipson came back to the room Jacob begged off and was dropped back home by Ben.

# Chapter 4

Rosie called him on his cell phone when he was working on the accounts at Jaya Electronics. The shop was owned by Rajesh, a Warbari. Though Jacob had a pathological dislike for Warbaris – he considered these unprincipled aliens nothing but vermin – Jacob realized that Jaya Electronics was the perfect cover for the accounts of the Movement. Neither the police nor the army – not even the intelligence – would ever suspect the accounts to be on their side of the fence. He had initially set up the accounts on a computer at the Ace Computer Training School where he taught software basics to school and college students. But he realized that if his cover were ever blown, that would be the first place they would go over with a fine toothcomb. When Rajesh the Warbari came to the computer center looking for help in setting up his business accounts on a newly purchased computer, Jacob quickly grabbed the opportunity himself instead of recommending one of his star pupils. Rajesh had even procured a Chinese made pirated version of a popular American accounting software. The arrangement was ironically symbiotic. All Warbaris kept two sets of accounts – the real and the fake. The fake (which Rajesh referred to as the "second") was the version for the government and it showed income at eighty percent below true profits. This was when Jacob grasped the enormity of the parallel economy the Warbaris were running. Even after the bribes paid to the politicians, the police and sometimes even the army, the profits they made were astronomical.

A fringe benefit was that Jacob came to know the names of those who were taking bribes on the sly. To see the names of some government officers (who also happened to be upstanding church elders) on the kickback list was initially a rude shock but it sadly confirmed how pervasive corruption had become in a tribal society that was once egalitarian and where leaders were once held directly accountable to the public. Western-style democracy had effectively killed the vibrant tribal democratic system that had flourished for generations at the grassroots level.

The main benefit, without a doubt, was the increased collections from the following month. Once he came to know the windfall profits the Warbari businessmen were making, the extortion demands made to them saw a steep rise. There was some half-hearted resistance initially. But the profits were still so high that the Warbaris quickly capitulated. But they also increased their prices to cover the additional payments they were forced to make and effectively passed on the payments to the public.

The fifteen thousand was paid out early in the morning before the banks opened. Jacob paid the messenger out of the cash he had got from Philipson the previous day. When the banks opened, he decided to draw fifteen thousand katas from another account and then deposit the forty thousand as a single deposit. That way it would be easier to track receipts later, he reasoned. The last thing he wanted was to be accused of misappropriation by those who knew nothing about accounting.

But Jacob had also done something he did not tell anyone else about. He had buried two hundred thousand katas in five hundred kata notes in a small tin box under the clump of banana trees in their backyard. The idealist that he was, it was not money stolen for himself but funds for meeting emergencies, especially during curfews imposed after skirmishes when banks could be closed for days on end. Or if the government ever froze their bank accounts this would cover the immediate expenses while they made new arrangements. He added notations to the accounts on the Jaya Electronics computer clearly indicating the location and the amount. Next to this tin box lay another smaller box, also of tin, containing the Chinese made pistol that he was issued with when he joined the cause. All his protestations of being a pacifist were brushed aside when he was told to keep it for self-defense or for committing hara-kiri if his cover was ever blown and he was close to being captured.

"Can you meet me at the cathedral in fifteen minutes?" asked Rosie.

"Are you in any kind of trouble, Rosie?" asked Jacob solicitously.

"No, I am fine. Just come."

On the way, he received another call. This time it was Philipson.

"They have agreed to release the bodies without a postmortem. It wasn't easy. But the government realized the public anger. Did you make the payment?"

"Yes, I did. He came at 7:00 a.m.," said Jacob.

"OK. Good. Talk to you later."

The massive wooden doors of the cathedral were closed but not locked. He pulled the heavy door open and quietly stepped inside. Coming in from the bright sunlight outside, it took a few minutes for his eyes to adjust to the subdued lighting inside. Only the electric candles near the altar were lit. The rest of the light came from sunlight streaming in through the high stained-glass windows. He looked around and saw the lone kneeling figure towards the center of the cathedral. Tiptoeing noiselessly, he reached the pew and quietly slid in. Rosie opened her eyes and gestured to him to wait. Jacob gazed up at the ornate ceiling and the expensive chandeliers brought from Rome. It was all breathtakingly beautiful, he had to admit. But palatial splendor was not something he easily associated with religion. True religion, he believed, was of the mind and the soul. Her prayer finished, Rosie sat up on the pew and turned to Jacob and smiled.

"Give me a few more minutes, please," she whispered.

"Take your time. I am in no hurry," said Jacob.

As they sat there side-by-side, alone in the quietness of the gigantic cathedral, the cares of the world seemed to fade away into distant memories. Wordlessly, Rosie placed her hand over his resting on the pew in the space between them. He turned his hand over and took her hand in his, their fingers intertwining. They sat that way for a long time, sharing once again the intimacy they had forsworn.

Then slowly disengaging her hand, Rosie said, "Let's go."

As they walked down the cathedral steps in the blinding sunlight, the noise of the traffic on the road below assailed their ears and it seemed to bring back with it the burdens that they had just left behind.

"I didn't know you were a closet Catholic," teased Jacob.

"I'm not. I'm still a Presbyterian – like you."

"Did you go to the priest for confession?"

"I know you are making fun of me," she said seriously. Then she stopped and turning to Jacob added gravely, "You and I will have a lot to confess when this whole business is over."

"Yes, we already have a lot to own up to. I fervently hope our battle will be short and swift and truth will triumph," said Jacob.

"Ever the idealist, aren't you? I come to this cathedral because it is so quiet and so very spiritual."

"I know what you mean. For a brief while in there I had forgotten about our struggle."

Before they reached the curb, they paused to talk about the previous day's shoot-out.

"I heard about it after I got home. It is terrible. Our land will soon turn into another Cambodia, Vietnam or Northern Ireland," said Rosie.

"That's my fear too. I wish there would be no violence, no lives lost. I wish our leaders would see the light and selflessly work for our tribe. And I hope the federal government will give us some amount of autonomy and not treat us like terrorists."

"Neither will happen automatically or easily, Jacob," Rosie said resignedly. "We need to fight and not give up. There will be a price to pay. There will be martyrs. It would all be worth it if we can change our society for the better."

"That's my hope too. Sometimes I have serious misgivings and doubts. I often wonder if I should just be passive like most people. But now I live from day to day, doing what is required of me."

"Are you going to the funeral?" asked Rosie.

"Yes, we must. Although I did not personally know any of the three we need to go to bid them goodbye. I just heard that the government has directed the commissioner to hand over the bodies to the families without a postmortem."

"That would be a huge relief to the relatives."

"Anyway, I got to run. We will be in touch," said Jacob holding out his hand.

"Goodbye, Jacob. Be careful."

With that, they walked the remaining steps down to the road and went in opposite directions.

***

The funerals were held on the third day as per the Somi custom. But in a break with tradition, a common public funeral service for all three dead young men was arranged in preference to separate funerals in their family homes. The whole Somi tribe grieved. Mixed with sorrow in equal proportion was also helpless wrath. Seething anger at the callous extermination of the defenseless young men. Nobody really believed the government version that the police fired in self-defense. Thanks to the efficient grapevine it was common knowledge that the police had planted the guns.

According to the tribal custom, a massive community meal was arranged for all who came to pay their last respects. Donations had poured in, both in cash and in kind. To the tarpaulin tent set up in a corner of the school soccer field were delivered sacks of rice, carcasses of beef and pork, bamboo baskets of vegetables, gunny bags of potatoes, tins of oil and even jeep loads of firewood. Volunteers were aplenty. While men cooked rice, meat and vegetables in big cauldrons over open fires, women cleaned the rice, dressed the meat and vegetables and prepared *kuwa*. Young girls wandered amongst the crowd serving tea and slices of cake. A group of young women volunteers sat on their haunches, next to four temporary iron drums set up to store water, washing the dirty dishes and sending them back for use.

By the time three o'clock had come around everyone had had lunch and had quietly assembled around the dais on the soccer field on which the three closed coffins had been placed. The religious service began with the singing of well-known hymns translated from English nearly a hundred years ago by missionaries. As one of the dead was a Catholic, the priest from his parish assisted the Presbyterian pastor in leading the service. After the prayers and the brief messages from the religious leaders of both denominations, it was time for eulogies. The principal of the college where two of the dead were students spoke cautiously, weighing his words carefully. Two other teachers also spoke followed by the headmen of the localities of the slain boys. It was at this point that the political bigwigs, as is their wont to be always late, arrived. In a different society, there may have been demonstrations of anger or hate but in the placid Somi way of life, such a reaction to authority would have been undignified and also disrespectful to the dead. So, when the Chief Minister Davidson Chapang and his cohorts walked down the center aisle to the front of the gathering there were only hushed whispers and snickers. But their looks did not conceal their venomous hate. When the young representative of the Sunday School spoke, he brought tears to many eyes. It was the turn of the president of the SSU, the Somi Students' Union, to speak and he lambasted the government, the police, and the army. Chief Minister Chapang tried to cover his embarrassment by pretentiously examining the *kuwa* with care. The local elected Member of Parliament spoke next, adroitly distancing himself from the government without seeming to be on the side of the rebels, whom he referred to as 'misguided nationalists'.

There was pin-drop silence when Chief Minister Chapang got up to speak. "Beloved families of the brave young men, fathers, mothers and young people," he said in a convincingly sad tone, "there is no sadness greater than the death of our children. There is no loss greater to a society than the untimely passing away of strong, able-bodied young men who are the future leaders of our land. We all grieve with the three families today. Who can comfort them? Only the Lord can. You and I, we are powerless mortals. We can only hope and pray that the Lord will wipe away the tears of the families and bring hope into their hearts. What a big tragedy this is for our society! How much bigger our tragedy will be if more of our men die this way? We, fathers and mothers, need to show our youth the right way. We need to instill in them our values and our vision for the future. We need them to take our land forward. They don't know what they are doing. Their intentions are good. But we have failed in our duty to guide them in the proper path. We need to constantly teach our youth the values of obedience, respect for authority, honesty and integrity ..."

Jacob could not take it any longer. "Honesty and integrity. What a hypocrite!" he muttered. "What an actor! He deserves an Oscar for making crocodile tears look so real."

He had had enough. He slowly extricated himself from the crowd that was standing within the periphery of the soccer field. The security guards of the Chief Minister and other Ministers were standing by their vehicles some distance away unconcerned with the ceremony.

Jacob looked back at the crowd to see if he could spot Rosie.

He could not and he walked home with a heavy heart.

## Chapter 5

Jacob was writing an article for the local newspaper on absentee government employees when his cell phone rang. It was Philipson.

"How are you doing? We haven't met for a week," said Philipson.

"I'm OK. It is good we don't meet every day. Our covers could be blown if we met too often," replied Jacob.

"Sau Jacob, there's something I want you to do today. How are you set for time?"

"Depends on how much time is needed," countered Jacob.

"Oh, not much. About an hour should be enough. What are you working on right now?" asked Philipson.

"I'm writing the anonymous article on absentee government employees that I told you about."

"Good! The one you wrote on the misuse of public vehicles by government officers was excellent. It taught them a good lesson."

"It was not the article, but the list the following week of names, car numbers, and the details of the private use of the government vehicles that scared the daylights out of them."

"Right! I remember that. They had thought the warning in the article was a joke. They didn't think anyone was watching them," chuckled Philipson.

"Without the help of the Somi Students' Union, we couldn't have done it. They covered every single one of those freeloaders!"

"That was good! Very satisfying! The public loved it too," said Philipson.

"You haven't told me what you want me to do today," reminded Jacob.

"Ah, yes. Remember the fellow who was arrested for murdering the pregnant girl in the woods? I am secretly informed that they are torturing him to get a confession. I think you are the best guy to intervene. You have always rooted for the underdog."

"Whether or not he actually committed the crime has to be proven in court. Right now, he is only the alleged murderer. Till it is proven he cannot be treated like a condemned criminal – let alone tortured. I will not allow that to happen," said Jacob vehemently.

"See? Didn't I tell you, you were the best person for this?" laughed Philipson.

"If they are torturing the guy, the police may not let me meet him."

"If that happens we will find another way. Give it a shot," said Philipson. "He is not at the main police station. They are working on him at the small north station."

***

Jacob did not wait long to go see the prisoner. The interruption had broken his chain of thought and he was also intrigued by the assignment he was given. He could not wait to right a wrong. The thought that every minute of delay might mean more torture for the hapless prisoner nagged him. After an early lunch, Jacob left the house and took a taxi to the police station. He got off some distance from the building and walked the rest of the way. The front yard of the station was packed with vehicles involved in accidents, almost all of them mangled beyond repair and left unclaimed by their owners. Why they couldn't remove these to some place out of town and not make the police station look like a junkyard was beyond him. The building itself was old and in poor repair. By the looks of it, it had needed a fresh coat of paint at least ten years ago, and the cobwebs around the eaves seemed to have been around even longer than that.

Jacob climbed the five steps to the narrow porch. The door was ajar and he could hear indistinctly someone shouting in the interior. Jacob knocked lightly at first and then more vigorously. The yelling stopped and he could hear footsteps approaching the front door. It was the fat and slovenly cop from the plains. He was in uniform sans the shirt and his fat belly covered by a dirty vest spilled out over the top of the trousers making the large belt buckle almost invisible. He looked disgustingly incompetent in the dirty sleeveless vest that was more yellow than white. To make matters worse, the policeman was somewhat out of breath and sweating profusely from some physical exertion.

Jacob had learned long ago to use language to his advantage. So instead of using the official national language of Dindi or English he spoke in his own Somi language. As he presumed, this put the alien policeman immediately on the defensive.

"Are you holding someone in custody here for murder?" asked Jacob coming straight to the point, dispensing with social niceties.

"Sir, the sub-inspector is not here," replied the policeman nervously.

"Who said I want to meet him? Did I mention his name?" asked Jacob feigning anger.

"No, sir," replied the policeman obsequiously, "But he is in charge."

"Where is he?" asked Jacob impatiently.

"He has gone to ..." the policeman suddenly stopped realizing that he may have gone too far.

"I know where he has gone," said Jacob looking at the watch on his left wrist. "He has gone to get his son from school, hasn't he?"

"I ... I don't know," murmured the policeman.

"You can tell him from me when he gets back that the SNLF will punish him if continues to misuse the government vehicle," said Jacob knowing that his surmise was correct. "Now, where is the prisoner?"

"Sir, I have to get orders from him," cringed the policeman.

"I don't care who you have to get orders from. I asked you a question and I need an answer. Or do you want me to take this to the Inspector General's office?" asked Jacob threateningly.

"No, sir. There is no need for that," groveled the policeman. "Why don't you come in?"

That was what Jacob was waiting for. He quickly stepped around the policeman reeking of sweat and headed straight for the two rooms at the back. The constable immediately realized his folly and tried in vain to stop him.

The first room was the sub-inspector's office. The table was piled high with papers and files. The grimy walls had notices stuck on them. The second room was the lockup. The cell door was open. Between the bars of the open door was stuck the khaki shirt of the policeman. The room had no windows. The unshaded light bulb in the center of the room was unlit. The only light in the room filtered in from the corridor through the iron bars of the cell. As his eyes adjusted to the reduced light he struggled to comprehend what he was seeing. It did not seem to have a face or head. When realization struck him, his mind and body recoiled in revulsion. The object in front of him was a spread-eagled human body strapped frontally against an iron frame. The stretched-out hands and legs were manacled to the rusted wrought-iron scaffold. The head was sunk forward on the chest and barely visible from the back where Jacob stood. The chained prisoner emitted low moaning sounds like an animal in distress. White-hot anger welled up within Jacob and everything turned red. Whirling around, he grabbed the burly policeman by the dirty vest and yanked him towards him.

With his face just inches away from the other man's, Jacob yelled, "You rotten scoundrel! How dare you treat a Somi like this? How dare you treat a human being like an animal? It is a crime to beat even an animal like this! How can you do this to another human being?"

"Orders ... orders from my boss," quavered the policeman, "I was only following orders."

"That's no excuse, you bastard! You don't have to obey an unjust order!" Jacob shouted, shaking his right fist menacingly.

"I have my family ... I need to support my family back home ..." pleaded the policeman, switching to Dindi, the national language.

"I don't care what your reasons are," hissed Jacob, staring unwaveringly into the policeman's eyes. "If you as much as raise a finger against a defenseless Somi tribal, you are dead meat. Make no mistake. The SNLF will get you."

"I ask for forgiveness ... I have nothing against your tribe ...I was ordered to get a confession out of him ..." said the policeman in a whimper.

Jacob suddenly had had enough. He released his hold on the vest and pushed the policeman away. He was equally disgusted with himself for losing his self-control. He also realized that he could be held guilty of assaulting a policeman but that did not bother him as much. As the policeman went to get his shirt from between the bars of the door, Jacob moved closer to the shackled captive. The bare back was crisscrossed with red welts. The thick cane lying on the ground had left parallel marks on the backs of the thighs and the calves. When Jacob walked over to the other side of the frame he was even more appalled by the savagery. The prisoner had clearly been used as a punching bag. The nose was bloodied. The upper and lower lips were cut.

Both eyes were blackened and the left eye had swollen shut.

"What did they do to you, Sau?" blurted out Jacob.

"Don't ask," came the hoarse whisper, barely audible. "They even gave me ... electric shocks ... yesterday ..."

"I am really sorry," said Jacob fervently. Then stepping closer to the man, he whispered in his ear, "The SNLF will protect you."

The man sighed but Jacob could not figure out if it was out of relief or resignation.

Turning around to the policeman who was buttoning his shirt up, Jacob said evenly. "You will treat your prisoner like a human being. Give him food and water when he is hungry or thirsty. Never beat him. Never! You understand?"

"Yes," said the policeman.

"You will treat all prisoners with dignity. If you do cruel things to anyone, you are a dead man. Remember that." He paused and repeated for emphasis, "Mark my words – you are a dead man."

With that, Jacob walked briskly out of the police station.

*** 

When Rosie arrived at the cantonment in the Commandant's jeep she was, as always, waved through the check-gate. The colonel was in high spirits in his office. Rosie winced as she feared the worst reasons for the colonel's gaiety. "Please, Lord, do not permit our people to be killed by this cold-blooded snake," she prayed inwardly.

"How is my beautiful young lady today?" asked Colonel Kattar rising from his chair. He did not come around the desk but leaned back in his high-backed chair and swiveled in either direction languorously.

"You seem to be very happy today, Colonel. How many undergrounds did you kill today?" asked Rosie with feigned nonchalance as she pulled back a chair and sat facing the colonel.

"We missed them by an inch – just a whisker. Next time they won't be so lucky. Their guts will be spilled out on the ground and their dead bodies will be eaten by the vultures of the forest," he said with a nasty smirk.

"Did you find their camp?" asked Rosie hoping her anxiety would not show.

"Did we find it?" laughed the colonel. "The fire was still smoldering! We found two abandoned car batteries. They must have been using them for radio communication. The heavy batteries would have slowed them down."

She realized that it must have been a close call. Either the unit had not broken camp as planned or the army had not gone in the direction suggested by her.

"I hope your men didn't burn down the village in frustration?" asked Rosie.

"No, they did nothing of the sort. But they had to whip the school teacher for challenging the captain," said the colonel unconcernedly.

Rosie groaned inwardly. "These fools lack cunning. They are so stupid to stand up against the army," she said to herself.

Aloud she said, "They think they are heroes!"

The colonel had a smug look on his face. Rosie knew that there was something else he was not telling her. She just hoped that the soldiers hadn't killed any men or raped any women.

"I have a surprise for you," the colonel said. "It is a present – just for you."

Rosie was unsure of how she should respond. The last thing she wanted was to accept some expensive gift and be indebted to this man she loathed. She had no desire at all to move this relationship to another level.

"I wasn't expecting a present today. It is not my birthday!" Rosie said with a nervous giggle and a shake of her shoulders.

"It doesn't have to be your birthday," he said as he pulled open the right drawer and placed a small battered cardboard box on the table. "We can celebrate your birthday again when it comes."

The colonel twirled the box with his right hand a couple of times before sliding it across the glass top of the table. Rosie did not like the gesture at all. She thought it exceedingly rude of him not to hand it over to her courteously. She did not pick it up till the colonel insisted, "Come on, take it! It's for you."

Rosie reached out with some reluctance and opened the box. She was dazzled to see a gold chain with an exquisite cross. Her irritation vanished in an instant. It was obvious that the necklace was not locally made. It lacked the garish ornateness of local jewelry. The elegance and simplicity of the design clearly pointed to its foreign origin.

"This is a big surprise. I am overwhelmed!" said Rosie unable to hide her joy. "Thank you very much!"

"I'm glad you like it. You will get more gifts as we become better friends."

Her smile disappeared in a trice. "Does he think he can buy with trifles?" she thought in anger.

Aloud she said, "Our tribal customs do not allow a woman to accept jewelry from a man unless they are formally engaged or romantically linked. We are not in either of those situations. I can keep this only if you let me pay for this."

"No, this is a gift! I cannot take any money from you," the colonel protested.

"In that case, I have to return this to you," said Rosie letting the gold chain slither through her fingers back into the box.

"How can I take money from you? I don't know the price."

"If you won't tell me how much you paid, let me give you a token price. It may not equal the actual price you paid, but my conscience would be clear."

"OK. If you insist, pay me ten katas," said the colonel.

"Ten katas? No, that is too low. I will pay you two hundred katas. That is still only a nominal price but I wouldn't be embarrassed to wear it."

The colonel continued to demur but Rosie would have none of it. She opened the black handbag she carried and took out two hundred kata notes and placed them on the table in front of the colonel.

"Thank you again for the necklace. I really like it," said Rosie. "In fact, I like it so much I will put it on right now."

"Do you want any help with that?" asked the colonel.

"No!" Rosie said in mock alarm, shaking her head vehemently. "That would be like you were marrying me."

The necklace really looked beautiful against her slender alabaster neck and the tiny cross sparkled against the burgundy colored top she was wearing.

"You look like a princess!" gushed the colonel.

"Thank you, Commandant," responded Rosie.

"I have one other surprise for you," said Colonel Kattar, clearly pleased that his present was so well received.

"No, I don't think I can take a second gift today! This necklace is enough gift for a year."

"No, no, it is not a present. Before I tell you what the surprise is, tell me, do you know the forest minister?"

"I have seen him at public meetings but I don't know him personally."

"Well ... I need your help. I need to find someone who knows the forest minister."

"Why?" asked Rosie.

"I need a teak permit," said the colonel bluntly.

"Since when have you started trading in teak wood?" asked Rosie with a laugh.

"The wood is for myself. I have enough teak for all furniture and even for all doors of my home. During the Minglai raid, we stumbled upon some cross-border smugglers. They were transporting teak wood down the Taiha river. They fled into the jungle when they saw the army."

"Did you kill them?" asked Rosie.

"Did I kill them? I was here! I had nothing to with the raid. It was the major who reported the incident. They found several foreign-made things stacked on top of the wood."

"Like what?" asked Rosie.

"You know, the usual. Gold bars, precious stones, currency ..."

"Including this necklace," completed Rosie.

The colonel was taken aback. He paused for a moment to consider whether to admit it or not.

Finally, he said, "How did you figure that out? Yes. The necklace too. The moment I saw it I knew it was perfect for you."

'You did not pay any money for this, you fake!' thought Rosie, remembering the incident of the empty scotch bottle.

It was whispered that soldiers were in cahoots with the smugglers and were making a fast buck. There were rumors going around that it went all the way to the top. Only the worst ever got posted to the Somi hills to fight the internecine war and they came only because of these hidden perks. Rosie knew by now that the colonel's words could not be taken at face value. She would need independent confirmation to find out the truth of the matter. Was the colonel himself a part of the smuggling ring? If not, did the smugglers abandon their spoils or were the goods confiscated? What was the fate of the smugglers? Were they alive or had they been killed?

"We can get a teak permit for you but it won't come free. You will have to pay some bribe to the minister," said Rosie.

"As long as it is reasonable, it's OK. If I were reselling this outside the province I could have given more," said the colonel.

"I will check and let you know. The uneasy relations between the federal army and the provincial government will make it difficult. But I will try," assured Rosie. In return, she knew, she could ask for a substantial pound of flesh at the right time.

Just then the orderly brought in a fresh bottle of whiskey. The colonel said something to the orderly and he went back to bring an empty bottle of Johnnie Walker and a funnel. Carefully watched by the colonel, the orderly transferred two-thirds of the cheap local whiskey to the empty scotch bottle and then he added water to top it up.

"I add water because the local whiskey is not as smooth as scotch," explained the colonel. After dismissing the batman, the colonel added, "My subordinates must see me as a man of class and distinction always drinking only imported scotch whiskey."

"You impostor! You cheapskate!" Rosie felt like yelling out, sickened by the colonel's duplicity. "Have you ever wondered what your orderly thinks of you, fobbing off cheap local whiskey as imported scotch to impress others?"

The colonel seemed totally impervious to his own double standards and tried to impress her. "There is one other thing I want to tell you. If you can get the teak permit for me I will take a two-week vacation to have the new furniture made and the doors put in."

"Will you accompany the teak home?" asked Rosie,

"Not really. I will follow the truck in my jeep till the inter-province border. Even with a permit, anything can happen if I am not there. I will use an army truck for this to make the passage easier through the check-gates and all the way to my home. After getting it across the border I will send the jeep back and travel by plane two days later. I plan to get to my hometown a day before the truck arrives there."

"Looks like you have it all planned out to the last detail," said Rosie.

"Of course! Do you know much the teak costs?" countered the colonel.

"No. How much?"

"At least two million katas. About forty thousand dollars," said the colonel with pride.

"And you got it for free. You did not pay even a single kata," said Rosie to herself. She realized that a two-week absence of the colonel could mean a significant break for the Somi National Liberation Front (SNLF).

"I just realized I have a contact in the government for the permit," said Rosie.

"You do?" asked the colonel rubbing his hands. "Who is it?"

"You don't need to know. But I will get you your permit," said Rosie with feigned bravado.

She could not stay longer. This was a big opportunity for SNLF. She had to let Jacob know right away.

The colonel, feigning drunkenness, tried more forcefully than on previous occasions to paw her and she had to thump his chest before he would let her go. In the scuffle, the top button of her blouse pattered to the ground. Rosie did not bother to pick it up. She grabbed her handbag and made a quick exit.

## Chapter 6

Jacob was happy with the increasing 'contributions'. But he wasn't sure if it was due to increased patriotism or due to the rising fear of the SNLF. In the preceding week, two drug traffickers had been publicly punished. They had to stand in front of the Secretariat building carrying a sign that said, 'I will not sell drugs again'. They had been warned that if they went back to drug dealing, they would be shot in their knees and if they still persisted, they would be executed. They knew the threats were not empty. Two pimps had met that fate right in front of the posh hotel from which they had operated.

The funding to the underground army had been stepped up. Jacob surmised that a major offensive was in the offing. He knew Philipson would tell him about it soon. His article on absentee government employees had appeared in the newspapers the previous Friday and had caused a huge stir. The embarrassed government issued a statement saying that employees who violated the rules of attendance would be punished. The press release also stated that supervisors would conduct surprise checks at outlying government offices. The Chief Secretary, the senior most government bureaucrat, called a press conference and sought the cooperation of village councils in identifying government employees who played truant. When asked if it was not the duty of the government he hemmed and hawed. But he stoutly denied that the press conference had been called in response to the newspaper article. "We are taking steps to ensure that we have a well-oiled and efficient government machinery," he said. On reading the newspaper report Jacob had wondered how the Chief Secretary could articulate such a barefaced lie with a straight face. Jacob thought that the divorce from reality could not be greater and the gulf between the rulers and the ruled wider.

As he was trying to decide whether he should call Rosie or not, his cell phone rang. It was Philipson and he wanted Jacob to come in right away for an urgent meeting. This was rather unusual because they usually met only after dark. Jacob figured something was up.

When he arrived at Philipson's house a short while later, Philipson was fit to be tied. He was raving and ranting and seemed to have gone berserk. The henchmen trio of Passa, Soma and Kamat were also present.

"We have to fight for our independence – for our freedom. If we don't, the Somi tribe will vanish from the face of the earth. We would be assimilated by the mainstream majority from the plains. The intermarrying has got to stop. We have to ban it!" he thundered pacing around like a caged panther. "Why do our women marry outsiders? Why? They look down on their own men because they say our men are drunkards. Men have no ambition. No money. Men are irresponsible. We need to reform. We have to go back to our old values. We don't want to be a part of this nation of beggars and thieves. We don't feel any patriotism for our nation. Our patriotism should only be for our tribe and for Somi Land!"

"Do you think our tribe can survive as an independent nation on its own?" asked Soma. "Without federal funding, can we survive?"

"What! You just don't get it, do you? You think only about the lucrative construction contracts that you get from the government. How many times have I told you that there are at least five countries in Europe that are smaller than us in area and in population? We don't have to remain chained to this neocolonial arrangement. Let us break free!"

"I am all for freedom and independence. But we could go the way of Cambodia if we don't watch it," interjected Jacob softly.

Philipson turned to him. "Independence requires maturity. We need to train ourselves and our people to be self-disciplined. If we do that there will be neither mayhem nor massacre. Our old political structures worked. We have to go back to our roots."

"I think we are all agreed on that. We want to preserve the traditions of our tribe. We want to preserve our tribe itself as a distant race. There cannot be two opinions about these. What is confusing me is the way we go about these goals," Jacob said.

"We have to fight. We have to stand up. If we don't, we will be overrun in no time like the Native Americans. Our land and our dignity will be snatched away from us. We will become self-destructing alcoholics like the Aborigines of Australia."

"OK, we are all agreed that we want to live with honor and we all want peace too. Anyway, what is the agenda for this meeting?" asked Jacob.

"Yes, the reason I called all of you is to tell you of the danger of selling ourselves. After our first uprising ten years ago, the federal government passed the so-called indigenous law to placate us. Only we can own our land. Outsiders cannot legally buy our land. And business licenses can only be issued to Somis. But look at what is happening. Outsiders are buying land and buildings. The choicest land and the biggest buildings are owned by them. Outsiders control all our businesses. Is it not true?" asked Philipson looking around the room.

Passa said venomously, "We are being duped. The violators should be thrashed."

"We have to be always vigilant. We also have to set standards for our people. Our politicians run after money. The people follow their example. Money and riches have become our gods," said Jacob.

"Well said, Sau Jacob!" commended Philipson. "We need to identify every business and each and every real estate transaction and bring the proxy culprits to book. Only then can we survive. Having a law in our favor alone will not save us."

"What actually happened?" asked Jacob.

"Look at the Fanais. We all know them. Their family is well respected. They are the aristocrats of our tribe. The parents have traveled to London and Paris and they are both well-educated. Look at their children. The son is a ne'er-do-well who plays video games all day and the three daughters have become harlots. The middle daughter applied for an industrial license to set up a cement factory. Everyone knows she is the kept woman of the Warbari businessman Krishan."

"The difficulty lies in proving that it is a proxy deal. How do we do that? These Warbaris are serpents. They cover everything. If you check the documents, you will find that she is the director or board member or something on that firm. That is legal," said Jacob.

"True. In the letter of the law what they are doing is lawful. But you and I know that it is all a sham. And being his mistress is shameful. Krishan is married to his Warbari wife and has children studying in college."

"I completely agree," said Jacob resignedly. "But what do we do?"

"I suggest that we instigate the Somi Students' Union to confront these proxy businesses. The Warbaris and the government are scared of the SSU."

"There is one problem," ventured Jacob.

"What's that?" asked Philipson annoyed.

"There's just two more months left for the annual exams. If they start this agitation now the students will suffer. As it is they are always behind the children of outsiders."

"Hmm," pondered Philipson for a while rubbing his chin. Then straightening up he said, "That's a risk we will have to take. We all need to make sacrifices."

Jacob made as if to reply but then changed his mind and stared at his hands.

"I haven't told you the worst thing yet," said Philipson dramatically. After looking around and confirming that he had everyone's attention he added, "Gloria sold her daughter to the Warbari."

"What?" asked Soma enraged.

"Yes, she did. All of us know how she got the money to build her palatial new home and buy the two imported cars. She has sold her name to Mahajan, the cunning old Warbari, for all his business licenses. She is his concubine. Last week she needed money for a shopping trip to Dubai and also to build an extension to the house. Mahajan did not need any new licenses. The crafty old lecher that he is, he asked Gloria to return later in the evening with her daughter to collect the money. And Gloria the shameless harlot did just that. She went back home alone with the money."

"Shameful! These harlots ought to be thrashed within an inch of their life," shouted Passa angrily.

"Yes, they need to be taught a lesson," said Soma and the others nodded in unison.

"But all this is nothing compared to what I have to tell you next," said Philipson, pausing for dramatic effect as he looked around the room. "The Director General of Police has committed a heinous crime."

"Who? Jasbir?" asked Jacob.

"Yes, him," answered Philipson. "He was brought in from outside our province by the government because of federal pressure. They said they couldn't trust a Somi in that position. And this fellow Jasbir is an immoral rogue. He has been stealing money given for undercover operations for which no accounts are needed. He uses his policemen to provide him women to satisfy his lust. He has taken bribes to hush up criminal cases. He has used police machinery to provide security and protection to Warbari businessmen and pocketed the money they paid. He has taken money from the rich to harass the poor and force them to sell their land."

"The federal government sends only the worst scum to our province," said Jacob despondently.

"He did the worst thing yet this last week. He summoned the wives of three prisoners on different days on the pretext of releasing their husbands. He then took each of them to his house and raped them. Next morning, he sent them home. He did not release the prisoners either."

"No! Tell me this is not true!" shouted Jacob jumping to his feet. "How dare he violate our women? This is an affront to our society!"

The raging fury of Jacob's response took everyone by surprise. Philipson walked over, held Jacob by the shoulders and gently eased him back into the chair.

"We will not let him go unpunished," said Philipson.

"He must be killed. We must not let him leave our land alive," said Jacob overcome by wrath.

"It is not easy. He is well-protected always. He moves around with a pilot car in front and an escort car behind, both with mounted machine guns. But we will find a way. He has gone too far this time. We will plan something with the SNLF to liquidate the bastard. Maybe a roadside bomb or something."

"Promise me one thing," said Jacob earnestly, rising from the chair and holding on to Philipson's arm.

"What?"

"I want to be part of that team. I don't care if it costs me my life, I want to see him killed before my very eyes," said Jacob with passion.

"OK. That can be arranged," said Philipson not very convincingly.

Kamat who had not uttered a word so far added, "I want to be there too. I want to kill a policeman in revenge for the deaths of our young men. And if that is the DGP, so much the better."

\*\*\*

Later that afternoon when Rosie came over to the house, Jacob led her out to the backyard and told her the whole story.

"My pacifist days are over. I am like a cornered cat now. I have to attack to survive. To preserve my sanity. To see justice meted out instead of injustice. The atrocities on our people can no longer be borne in silence. Even the stones will cry out if we remain silent and do nothing."

"I admire your zeal, Jacob," said Rosie softly as she held her hand to his face. Jacob put his hand over hers and pressed her hand tightly to his cheek.

"Our lives are forever changed," said Jacob looking into her eyes.

"Yes, a terrible beauty is born," she murmured inaudibly.

"What?" asked Jacob but she did not repeat herself.

"It's nothing," she said as they moved back into the house for tea.

"That's a beautiful gold chain you have there," remarked Jacob when he noticed the new necklace. "Is it from your new beau or a secret admirer?" he asked playfully.

"No, you know that cannot be true!" she replied. "It was given as a present but I paid something for it. I didn't want to be obligated to the giver."

Jacob decided not to pry any further and let the matter drop.

Ma had prepared an elaborate afternoon tea with devilled eggs, curried beef and a small bowl of rice. The tea itself was a delightful blend of milk, sugar, and freshly brewed orange pekoe tea.

What made the tea special was the presence of Edwin. He did not have extra classes that afternoon and was home early. Edwin sat quietly in the circle with the gangly ungainliness of adolescence, his hair neatly brushed to the side and his ears alert to every nuance of the conversation of the elders. He held his older brother in such awe that it completely masked his affection. His brother was the smartest, most intelligent human being he knew. Edwin did his best to emulate his brother's orderliness, his attention to detail and his mannerisms. Edwin practically venerated his brother.

"Here, have one more devilled egg," offered Rosie and Edwin picked one up, shyly murmuring his thanks. Likewise, only when Ma offered him did he take some more curried beef and rice.

"How well do you know the Minister for Forests & Environment?" asked Rosie sipping her tea.

"Is the tea sweet enough?" asked Ma.

"Yes, Ma, the tea is delicious!" said Rosie.

"What do you want with the Minister of Forests?" asked Jacob not looking up from his bowl.

"Let's say, I need a favor," said Rosie mysteriously.

"It depends on what kind of favor you are looking for," said Jacob unamused.

"OK. What if I need a log permit?"

"A log permit? What are you into now? Timber smuggling?"

"No, it is not for me. It is for a friend ... not a friend actually but let's say a business acquaintance," said Rosie smiling.

"Let me guess. Is this person in business?" asked Jacob.

"No, not business. But I have business connections with him."

"It is a 'he', is it?" asked Jacob playfully.

"Ma, I will go out to play," said Edwin rising.

"OK, don't be late," said Ma.

"Bye, Nau Rosie! Bye, Aga!" said Edwin respectfully before darting out of the kitchen.

"Yes, the person is a male," said Rosie after Edwin had left the room.

"Is the permit for transporting logs to another province or is it for use within the province?" asked Jacob deadpan.

"For moving them to another province."

"Then I think I know who your business partner is," said Jacob with a twinkle in his eye.

"I'm sure you don't. But go ahead and guess if you want to," said Rosie smiling smugly.

"It is the Commandant, isn't it?" asked Jacob with a faint smile.

Rosie blanched and nearly dropped her cup.

"How did you guess that?" asked Rosie shocked.

"Let's go out for a walk," suggested Jacob. "Ma, I will be a little late tonight."

When they were outside and clear of the house, Jacob turned to Rosie.

"You thought nobody knew, didn't you? You thought nobody saw you enter the Secretariat from one gate and exit the other and then get into the waiting army jeep?" asked Jacob.

"How did you know all this?" asked Rosie in disbelief.

"Don't get me wrong. I am not spying on you. But the 'company' keeps close tabs on everyone. You are watched closely. All of us are. But there is nothing to worry about. You are clean."

"This is unbelievable!"

"I'm sorry if this has upset you. We are doing dangerous work and we need someone watching over our shoulders," Jacob said conciliatorily.

"Do we? Speak for yourself. I don't."

"If it'll make you feel any better, I'm under surveillance too. I found that out early."

"I wish you had told me," said Rosie accusingly.

"Don't get me wrong. I wasn't informed about all your movements. I followed you myself one day just to find out if you had a new boyfriend."

That seemed to soften Rosie up. "I cannot fall in love with someone new. I already told you that. But you love our cause more than you love me."

"That's not true. It is just that one cannot afford to have hostages in this battle. And you agreed to work for the same cause. Our independence. Our freedom."

"That's true. Just know that I still love you and there is no other. I thought I would not tell you that till it was all over. But there you have it."

"I love you too, Rosie," said Jacob holding open his arms.

"I can't hug you here in the open! Are you crazy?" Rosie laughed.

"Love does strange things to you," said Jacob smiling.

"I have the perfect name for you," said Rosie mischievously.

"Why, what's wrong with Jacob?"

"Nothing. But your new name is Strelnikov. Sounds exotic, doesn't it?" said Rosie smiling. "From now on you are Jacob Strelnikov."

"Where did you get that name from? Sounds Russian."

"Yes, it is Russian. It's from Pasternak's Dr. Zhivago. It is the name of the idealist Red Army partisan who left his wife and child behind to fight the White Army."

"He must have been a tough character."

"He was. You must read the book. Or see the movie with Omar Sharif and Julie Christie."

"I will. Regarding the permit you wanted, I think I might be able to get it for you," said Jacob.

"Really? That would be wonderful!" gushed Rosie.

"Since I now know your source, I will tell you mine. There is a mole in Chief Minister Chapang's office," said Jacob quietly.

"No way!" exclaimed Rosie.

"It is kind of surprising but it's true. I will let you know tomorrow when I can get that license for your business associate."

"Thank you, Strelnikov!" And then after a pause, she added, "That name really suits you."

## Chapter 7

Ma was very anxious when she heard a knock on their door after midnight. When Jacob walked to the front door and asked who it was before opening the door, he discovered it was Ben, Philipson's driver.

"It's OK, Ma. It is Sau Ben, my friend. You can go back to sleep," called out Jacob as he opened the door. But Ben would not come in, saying it was too late.

"Sau Philipson asked me to give this to you," Ben said holding up a large discolored cloth bag. "It is money."

"Why did he have to send it at this time of the night?" asked Jacob.

"There will be payments to be made very early in the morning. He wants you to put the rest in the bank."

After Ben left, Jacob emptied the cloth bag on the low central table. There were sixteen bundles of currency with small slips tucked under the rubber bands stating the amounts held back by Philipson. The bulk of the notes were five hundred kata but there were also a few hundred and thousand kata notes as well. Jacob spent the next hour checking the bundles and totaling them up on a sheet of paper. Philipson had retained twenty-two thousand out of a total of three hundred eighty-four thousand katas. This was a huge jump in collections and Jacob suspected again that something big was in the offing. With the money was also an envelope in his name. When he opened it, he found half a ten kata note with an uneven, jagged edge where it had been cut in the middle.

Jacob knew what that was for.

***

Next morning over morning tea, Ma questioned Jacob about the midnight caller.

"Ma, don't worry about it. It was a business matter. Sau Ben wanted me to do some work for him today," said Jacob looking down into his cup.

"What kind of work is it that comes in the middle of the night? Can't it wait till morning?" Ma asked putting the kettle back on the fire.

"Ma, you have to trust me. It was something important. It could not wait till morning."

"You always told me the truth before, son. Now you've begun to hide things from me," Ma said matter-of-factly.

"I still will not tell you a lie, Ma. But there are business details of others that I have to keep to myself."

"You have told me that excuse before. I still think you are not being completely honest with me," Ma said.

"It is only other people's secrets that I hold back. I may not tell you everything but I will not tell you a lie, Ma," said Jacob gently.

"I have to believe you. What else can I do? Let me tell you about something else. If you have time, please go to the house of Nau Olivia today. You know she has been unwell for nearly two months now. They have decided to take her outside the province to Ultapur in the hot plains for treatment."

"OK, Ma, I will go and see Nau Olivia today. When are they taking her to Ultapur, do you know?" asked Jacob.

"I think it is next Monday. They have arranged the ambulance from the locality's welfare society. Give Nau Olivia's daughter some money on our behalf. I don't know how they will afford all the expenses."

"I will give them some money, Ma, on your behalf. I need to go now and finish the work I was given last night," said Jacob.

"Don't do anything dishonorable, son. Always try to keep yourself blameless and untainted."

"I will, Ma," said Jacob rising.

Just then Edwin came in carrying his school bag over his shoulder and his shoes in his hands.

"Edwin's exams start today," said Ma.

"What subject do you have today?" asked Jacob.

"English paper one. Tomorrow is English two," said Edwin pulling on his socks.

"Here, buy some eats after the exam," said Jacob holding out a ten kata note.

"Thank you, Aga," said Edwin, his face lighting up in a big smile.

***

Jacob hurried to the bank anxious to put the money away safely. He had stuffed the bundles in different pockets of his black leather jacket, hoping no telltale bulges would be visible. As it turned out he was too early. The bank always opened late. "Punctuality was never one of our strong points," said Jacob to himself.

He was startled when he felt a tap on his shoulder and a man whispered from behind in a low voice, "Excuse me."

Jacob turned around sizing up the interloper. He was young, in his late twenties or early thirties and wore a black leather jacket like most young men his age.

"Yes?" asked Jacob warily.

"Sorry for intruding in this manner. Are you Sau Jacob?" asked the stranger hesitantly.

"Yes, that's my name. What can I do for you?"

"Can we talk privately?" asked the young man, clearly relieved.

"OK. Let us go to the parking lot across the road," suggested Jacob.

When they had dodged the two-way traffic on the road and were on the other side, the young man looked around to be certain they were out of earshot of anyone and said sotto voce, "I'm an emissary of the Chief Commander."

Jacob's intuition had proved right again.

"You need to give me the token," said Jacob.

"Of course!" said the agent extricating with some effort a piece of paper from a secret slit in the lining of his jacket.

Jacob took out the piece of the ten kata that he had received along with the money. The two matched perfectly. On the small piece of paper was written in a clear, legible hand: 'Pay the bearer the sum of two hundred and fifty thousand katas', below which was a crude rubber stamp with a pair of crossed swords between two arcs reading 'SNLF' and 'Somi Land'.

"I can't count the money here in the open. Shall we go to a restaurant somewhere nearby?" asked Jacob.

"No, it's not safe. Let me think." The courier gripped his forehead with his right hand, shielding his eyes. Then seeming to make up his mind he pulled out his cell phone and whispered briefly something inaudible.

"You can count the money in the safety of my jeep," he said brusquely.

An uneasy lull in the conversation followed with neither knowing what to say. After a few interminable minutes, the messenger turned to Jacob and said gravely, "We need more volunteers—especially girls. They are viewed less suspiciously by the security forces."

Jacob wasn't sure if he was trying to recruit just him or whether he wanted Jacob to actively recruit others for the SNLF underground army.

"Are we launching a big offensive?" asked Jacob.

"Not necessarily soon. That is going to take time and we need to be ready," answered the messenger.

The jeep soon arrived and in its covered confines Jacob counted out two hundred fifty thousand katas and handed it over after taking a signed acknowledgment on the demand note. A brief shake of hands and the transaction was complete.

The bank was open now. The crowd that had been waiting outside had all moved indoors. Jacob quickly crossed the street and deposited the balance of one hundred thirty-four thousand katas.

***

When Jacob called Rosie after three o'clock in the afternoon the heat of the midday sun was already wearing off.

"Would you like to come with me to Nau Olivia's house?"

"Gladly. But what for?" asked Rosie.

"Ma told me she has been ill for some time and is going to be taken to Ultapur for investigation and treatment. We ought to go and see her," said Jacob.

"Of course. What time?"

"How about in an hour and a half?" suggested Jacob.

"We have been seeing each other almost every other day these past two weeks. People will think we are together again," laughed Rosie.

"Aren't we? They don't know that our romance is on hold. Nobody does except us," retorted Jacob lightly.

"And even we don't seem to be sure!" said Rosie dryly.

"Meet me at the Zareta Bakery at five," said Jacob.

Jacob took a taxi home and after tea with Ma took a brief siesta. He was tired. The errands to the bank and government offices had taken their toll. The inefficiency and the callous bureaucracy always rankled. "When will we abandon corruption and catch up with the West in efficiency? If Singapore can do it, why can't we?" he asked himself. But when he took out the teak transport permit from the jacket pocket, the irony did not escape him. Had the government been totally rule-bound he could never have obtained that permit for Rosie. All he had to do was meet the Principal Private Secretary to the Chief Minister. Although only a middle-level civil servant he wielded tremendous power because of his position. The other ministers fawned on him because of his proximity to the Chief Minister. Even if in private they referred to him sometimes as an 'extra-constitutional authority', no one voiced this opinion in public for fear of retribution. As it turned out the Principal Private Secretary was Jacob's mole. Their friendship went back to their Christian Endeavor days and the many times that Jacob had come to his aid in high school. Their friendship was so ardent that their Sunday School teacher had once referred to them as David and Jonathan. Though their career paths had diverged, they still shared an intense love for their land and their brethren and a strong bond of friendship. With such a powerful ally, getting the permit was mere child's play. The Principal Private Secretary had picked up his phone and called the Private Secretary to the Minister for Forests and after exchanging pleasantries had disarmingly requested the teak permit to be obtained from the Forest Minister. When there was a slight hesitation at the other end, it was cunningly implied that the permit was needed at the highest level and it was needed 'right now'. By the time Jacob had finished the tea served by a uniformed _peon_ (low-ranking attendant), the permit had been delivered in a sealed envelope.

"Be sure to enter the registration number of the truck. That information has been left blank," was all the Principal Private Secretary said as he handed over the permit.

From the Secretariat, he had gone to Jaya Electronics and updated the accounts with the day's deposits and payments. He had to go back to the Secretariat to find out the status of the government scholarships for students passing the high school exam. There were many allegations of nepotism and bribery. The Education Department was not particularly helpful. He did not have any contacts there. After making little headway against the wall of bureaucracy, he decided to go home and try a different tack the next day.

"They need to be taught a lesson," he said to himself as his drowsiness overcame him and he slipped into a fitful doze.

*** 

On waking up a short time later, Jacob had another cup of tea and then caught a taxi to the Zareta Bakery. Rosie arrived a short time later. After buying a cake and bottle of Horlicks as presents for Nau Olivia, they decided to walk instead of taking a taxi.

When they reached the house, there were other visitors who had arrived earlier. Nau Olivia lay unmoving, staring at the ceiling. Her daughters rushed about bringing tea and cookies for the visitors. Her husband sat quietly aloof on a settee in the corner.

"What did the doctors say?" asked Jacob gently after the initial small talk and tea.

"They could not find out the problem. They kept giving us different medicines for her headache but that only made her worse. It has been six weeks now," said the husband resignedly.

"They told you finally to take her to Ultapur?"

"Yes, they told us they have modern machines there and better doctors in that province."

"The government doctors told you this?" asked Jacob.

"Yes. We also consulted private doctors but they said the same thing. Many of them are also government doctors making money on the side," said the husband unable to conceal his disillusionment.

"How will you transport Nau Olivia to Ultapur?" asked Jacob.

"If it weren't for the Somi Students' Union we would perish. They have lent us their ambulance. We only need to put in the fuel. The government ambulances were not available."

"I know why they aren't available," chipped in Rosie. "In the mornings and evenings, they use them as school buses for their children and the drivers treat them like their own private cars when the doctors are not using them. They even use them for staff picnics!"

"It is like climbing a greasy pole," said Jacob. "One foot up, two feet down. When that newspaper article was published, they all seemed to be scared to death. Now it is as if they don't care anymore."

"A few of them must be given exemplary punishment so all would learn," said Rosie.

"We don't know how much the treatment will cost. We are poor people. We have mortgaged our rice fields," said the husband despairingly. "Without the help of our neighbors, we would die."

"Here, keep this," said Jacob pressing an envelope into the husband's hands. "Keep it as a gift from my mother."

Jacob's anger boiled over when they were outside.

"Our politicians will burn in hell for their greed. They siphon off the federal funding for health for their own selfish desires. The common man then has to sell his home and hearth to get medical treatment in another province. In effect, the politicians are sucking the blood of the poor."

"How do we hold them accountable? Nobody seems to care," said Rosie.

"I am not going to give up. My next article for the papers will be on the healthcare mess. Even the medicines are fake. At best, they are harmless placebos. At worst, they maim and kill. And yet the crooks get away scot-free. This cannot go on."

They hailed a share-taxi that was not full and squeezed themselves against the passengers that were already in. When they were nearing their locality Jacob's phone rang. It was Philipson. "I'm in a taxi right now. I will call you soon," said Jacob disconnecting the phone quickly.

Immediately after alighting from the taxi, Jacob returned Philipson's call.

"He's dead – dead in custody. The police are calling it a suicide. But it is murder by the state," Philipson's voice quivered in rage.

When Jacob conveyed the news to Rosie in the deepening dusk, the horror of this hideous act seemed to sap them of all their strength. It seemed only natural to cling to each other, Jacob's hand gently caressing Rosie's head and her tears coursed uncontrollably down his shirtfront as she pressed her face against his chest.

"They have turned into ogres ... lost all humanity," said Jacob bitterly.

Rosie had dinner that night at Jacob's house, with Ma, Jacob, and Edwin. The meal was a somber affair after Jacob related what had happened. While sipping light black tea afterward, Jacob took out the envelope containing the permit and handed it to Rosie.

She could not believe her eyes. She looked in amazement at Jacob and cried with delight, "How did you do this? This is a miracle!"

Jacob merely smiled enigmatically. He had not seen her so happy in a long while. After Ma had handed out *kuwa* to everyone, Jacob walked Rosie to the road.

## Chapter 8

When Colonel Kattar received the permit the next day, he could not hide his glee. He practically leapt, out of his chair, attempted an inelegant two-step and then tried to catch Rosie in a bear hug, which she deftly dodged.

"This is wonderful! This is incredible!" he blurted out and then he let out some more exclamations in an unidentifiable language that Rosie could not decipher.

"You deserve a big prize for this. Tell me what you want and I will give it to you."

"Nothing, Colonel. I need nothing from you personally. Except what it cost me. Thank you all the same," said Rosie modestly.

"You don't realize what a big accomplishment this is. Wait till the teak gets to my home. Then you will see the reaction of my neighbors," said the colonel dreaming of the opulence the teak would add to his home and the higher status that he would rise to socially.

"Well, there is one thing you can do," said Rosie gravely. "Please treat my people with respect and dignity. Treat our freedom fighters according to the principles of the Geneva Convention. Put an end to killing my people in cold blood."

"This is war," remonstrated Colonel Kattar.

"This is not war. We are a part of your country. Why does the federal government treat us like enemies? I know you are obeying orders. All I am asking you is to treat prisoners and civilians humanely. Nothing more, nothing less," said Rosie evenly.

"I have done my best, my dear. But, for your sake, I will try even harder."

"Promise?" she asked.

"Word of honor."

She did not know what it was worth but she thought it was at least something.

"You have no idea what I had to go through to get this permit for you," said Rosie piling on the guilt.

"Didn't you tell me you will have to pay some *baksheesh* (bribe) for this?" asked the colonel.

Rosie scrambled to do some mental arithmetic. One percent of two million (the value the colonel had quoted) was twenty thousand katas. She decided to go with it.

"Twenty thousand katas."

"Twenty thousand? Isn't that too much?" asked the stingy colonel.

"How is it too much? The teak is worth two million. The forest department demanded fifty thousand katas. I had to do a lot of bargaining to bring it down to forty, thirty and finally twenty."

"Do you think they will settle for ten? Or fifteen?" asked the colonel haggling.

Rosie decided not to budge. The money would add to the coffers of the revolution. She was inwardly amused to think that the colonel would unwittingly be funding the very same forces he was waging a war against. In fact, she figured he could be the biggest individual donor after the filthy rich Warbari businessmen.

"No way. That is not negotiable. If we don't pay the twenty thousand your teak logs could be seized at the check-gate and you will end up paying much more."

The colonel unhappily scratched his stubbly jaw.

"All right, I will pay you the twenty thousand with my money now. After I return I will recover it through some cooked-up truck repair bills."

"This fellow is an out-and-out crook," said Rosie to herself.

Colonel Kattar left the room to return a short while later with a leather briefcase. Very deliberately he took out two bundles of one hundred kata notes and casually tossed them on the table.

"Here you are," said the colonel gruffly.

"Thanks!" said Rosie as she picked up the crisp new bundles and dropped them into her handbag. "But this doesn't release you from your solemn promise," she reminded the colonel.

It seemed for a brief moment that the colonel had forgotten but he quickly caught on. "The Geneva Convention and all that. Of course, of course. I will do something when I get back. I will brief the officers at the monthly meeting or something."

"I am glad I could help with the permit. I'm sure you will help me too when I need your assistance."

"Of course! Any time! You only have to let me know. I will place the whole army machinery at your disposal. Feel free to come to the officers' club anytime you like – even when I am gone on my two-week furlough with the teak. I will tell my adjutant to send you a vehicle whenever you need," said the colonel loftily.

"I think I will take you up on that. If there is one thing I need, it is some form of transport most of the time."

Little did she realize then how prophetic her words would turn out to be.

"How about a kiss before you go?" asked the colonel with a wink.

"I got you the permit!" Rosie said faking gaiety and edging quickly to the door.

"I will be away for two weeks," said the colonel with a pleading look.

"Have a good trip. And good luck with the renovation," said Rosie as she quickly slipped out.

***

Later that evening, she told Jacob, "It is my turn to surprise you." Then, taking the two bundles of currency out with a flourish, she declaimed theatrically, "And now the outstanding contribution to our cause – twenty thousand katas for our noble mission! From the chief lackey of the federal government who torments us the most!"

"Who gave you this? You got this from the army?" asked Jacob incredulously.

"Yes. From Colonel Kattar, the Commandant, no less."

"How did you manage that?"

"I told him I had to grease the palms of the government *baboos* (office clerks) to get the permit. He tried to bargain but I stuck to my guns," said Rosie matter-of-factly.

"Excellent!" exclaimed Jacob.

"Not only that, I got him to promise to respect the human rights of our soldiers captured in combat. I have also been granted increased access to the army facilities. Soon I will take you on a picnic in an army jeep," she said laughing.

For some reason, Jacob did not share the levity of the remark. He seemed to be lost in thought. Then, an enigmatic smile crossed his face. The brainwave spurred him into action. He stood up suddenly to his full height and said, "You have just given me an amazing idea. I have to go. Sorry to leave you so abruptly, but this is important."

When he reached the door, he turned back to say, "And thanks for getting that donation!"

With that, Jacob was gone.

Rosie was puzzled but she was not new to Jacob's sudden bursts of lateral thinking. She knew he would come back to tell her all about it. She was always the first one he shared his brilliant brainwaves with.

But this once she was wrong.

\*\*\*

When Jacob arrived, the meeting was already in progress. Kamat was absent today.

"That Captain must be killed," Soma was saying. "It is an insult to our tribe."

The issue, Jacob quickly discovered, had to do with the evening parties that the Governor's aide-de-camp, a junior army officer, threw for the stenographers and young female clerks of the Secretariat during curfew hours. The captain had an endless supply of beer, gin, whiskey and rum and an array of scrumptious delights from the Governor's kitchen. As a matter of fact, it was the bearer of the food from the kitchen to the party-room that leaked the news. He had seen young women dancing in gay abandon and some of them were in various stages of undress and he reported this to a friend of Soma. Soma had personally questioned one of the women that the bearer had recognized. She had vehemently denied doing anything inappropriate. She had told him that evenings confined to one's house during periods of curfew were boring. She said it was only music, dancing, and good food but she did admit to drinking. Soma had let her off with a warning of dire consequences if she or her friends went there ever again.

"He has outraged the modesty of our young girls and he must be killed," Soma insisted.

"Are you sure he raped any of the women? He doesn't sound anything like the DGP Jasbir," said Passa.

"Nevertheless, he must be taught a lesson. He is an outsider and an army officer. They should not touch our women. And our women also should know better. Killing the captain will send the right message," Soma insisted.

"I am not so sure. The punishment must fit the crime. Think also of the repercussions. The army will launch a merciless attack. Our civilians will suffer. Moreover, we have more serious issues to deal with. Jasbir, for example," remonstrated Jacob.

"They both need to be punished," Soma insisted. "It does not have to be one or the other. We can kill both."

"We would be unleashing a wave of terror upon ourselves if we are not selective. I say we deal with the DGP first," said Jacob.

"I'm going to intervene here," said Philipson who had been silently watching the discussion so far. "Let us keep assassinations aside for the time being. Both the targets you have in mind are high profile people and it will not be easy. There is a high likelihood that their security will thwart our attempts and, even if we were successful, our agents may have to pay the ultimate price. Remember, neither of them is a soft target."

"There is something else that I want to discuss," continued Philipson. "This has to do with business. These Warbaris still have a stranglehold on us. Even after we passed the law prohibiting outsiders to do business in our land, they have circumvented the law by forming partnerships with our tribal brethren."

"Didn't we discuss this the last time?" asked Jacob.

"Yes, we did. We wanted the Somi Students' Union to launch an agitation but you said their exams were near. I thought we shouldn't let that delay us but later I thought you had a point. We will wait till their exams are over," said Philipson.

"Thank you," said Jacob.

"The issue we are discussing now is slightly different. Six of our richest families – and their Warbari partners – control our economy. They are monopolies. Be it petroleum, rice, cement, cars, packaged milk, sugar, cooking oil ... there is no competition. They are raking in abnormal profits. How can we spread the wealth more evenly?"

"I know nothing about how the economy works," said Soma with an uneasy laugh.

"Me neither," said Passa. "I am a man of action."

"We are not discussing academics here," said Philipson with a touch of exasperation. "I am talking about making our society more equal. Like it was before."

"I think the tribal homogeneity we once had is lost forever. It is too late for communism. Socialism might work, but we need a visionary leader. We don't have one at the moment," said Jacob.

"There must be some way to compel them to take in more partners or something?" asked Philipson.

"It cannot be enforced. The companies are legal entities. And even if we did, that would not solve the problem. How many partners can they take on, if at all they agree to it? Just a few more rich people while the majority will continue to be poor."

"So, nothing can be done?" countered Philipson.

"Several things can be done. The government could break up the monopolies. Other producers and suppliers from outside could be encouraged to enter our territory with new local partners. The big trading houses could be taken over by the state. Or at least they could be converted to public companies with many shareholders instead of just a single owner. The bare minimum they can do is lower abnormal profits to reasonable levels."

"This is more complicated than I thought," said Philipson wearily, slapping his forehead. "I am going to meet the six richest Somi businessmen next week."

The meeting had already ended for Soma and Passa. They were swilling rum they had pinched from the corner table. That they were discussing matters less profound was obvious from the manner in which they were guffawing and slapping their thighs totally oblivious to their surroundings.

Jacob looked at the two of them sitting on adjacent sofas at the far corner of the room, diagonally across from him and Philipson. And then he glanced at Philipson on the adjoining sofa. For a moment, he seemed undecided. Then quickly making up his mind, he gestured Philipson to lean over.

Jacob moved closer too so their heads were over the small corner table.

Then he whispered, "I will take on the job of killing the Director General of Police, Jasbir."

"What?" recoiled Philipson startled.

"I will kill the DGP," said Jacob evenly without any trace of emotion.

Philipson knitted his brows in thought and sat back on his sofa. Then pulling himself to his feet, Philipson gestured Jacob to follow him to the next room.

"What did you say just now?" asked Philipson a trifle testily.

"I know you are surprised. You may even think I have lost my mind. But I have carefully thought about it. I have a plan. And right now, it is only a plan. But I think it is a plan that will work. I am willing to take charge of the elimination of Jasbir the DGP."

"Are you crazy? You are a pacifist. At least that is what you told me. Now you want to kill someone. That too, someone who is in the highest security bracket. This is suicide!"

"I know it sounds crazy. And yes, I was a pacifist. But I have changed. I cannot sit idly by and watch iniquity after iniquity being piled on our people. The time has come for me to act. Our own people are in disarray. The lure of wealth has blinded them. It is no longer us versus them – our tribe against the rest of the world. It has now become also us versus us. Evil cannot be allowed to thrive unfettered. I am willing to take the risk," said Jacob.

"I admire your courage. But do you realize that you might be killed?" asked Philipson, still unable to believe what he was hearing. "You are being foolhardy."

"I am fully aware of the risk. I might be killed. But I am not a suicide killer. I don't want to die. If my plan works I will not have to die."

"You realize that you will be committing murder, don't you?" asked Philipson.

"Yes, I have thought about that too. As a Christian, I wish I didn't have to do it. But desperate situations require desperate remedies. Even Moses killed an Egyptian. Jasbir to me is the incarnation of all evil. If anyone deserves to die, it is he."

"OK," said Philipson taking a deep breath and exhaling. "What do you want me to do?"

"Nothing right now. I will let you know," said Jacob.

"But what is your plan? How will you kill someone who is surrounded twenty-four hours by armed police guards?" asked Philipson.

"Right now, it is only a plan. I will share it with you on an as-needed basis. Let me work out the details."

"I cannot believe this. My brains trust is taking up arms to kill. And he doesn't even trust me!" said Philipson shaking his head in disbelief.

"I don't want to hide anything from you. You are my boss. I will tell you everything at the right time. But there is nothing I can tell you now – except I have this deep desire to seek retribution for the brutality inflicted on our young men ... to avenge the dishonor of our women ... to redeem our tribal dignity and honor. That is all I want."

Philipson stared at Jacob for a long time, his expression a blend of admiration and puzzlement.

"I thought you were my accountant and strategist," he said shaking his head. "I thought I knew you."

## Chapter 9

The colonel left five days later and not the very next day as he had hoped. It took four days of intense cajoling by the colonel to get his leave sanctioned. He had to cook up some story about his wife being ill before his request was granted by army headquarters.

As he rode in his jeep with the covered truck following closely behind, several pairs of eyes watched his progress from various vantage points of the town, although it was only five thirty in the morning and the colonel thought the whole town was asleep.

At the border check-gate, the profusely sweating and flustered colonel was relieved when the forest guards finally waved him through after nearly an hour of waiting. It was a transformed and triumphant Colonel Kattar who drove to the nearest airport.

"They thought they would ruin me with this posting? Pshaw! I will beat them at their own game and return richer than any of my batch-mates holding prized postings. I can wring water out of a stone! And turn copper into gold!" crowed the colonel as the jeep (now unimpeded by the slow trailing truck) increased its speed and raced towards the airport.

***

"Are you not going to church today, son?" asked Ma during the morning tea.

Edwin looked down into his cup as Jacob considered the question.

"It has been three weeks since you went to church with us," added Ma reprovingly.

"OK. All right. I will go," said Jacob with a cheerfulness that surprised Ma and Edwin.

"Did you hear about the miracle of Nau Olivia?" asked Ma stirring the boiling rice in the aluminum vessel.

"No, what happened?" asked Jacob.

"She is completely alright! She can walk about and talk and laugh. They came back yesterday afternoon from Ultapur." Said Ma.

"That is a miracle. When I went to see her, I had my doubts if she would survive the road trip to Ultapur in the plains," said Jacob munching on a slice of buttered bread and sipping hot tea.

"Here the doctor was saying it was brain cancer but there they discovered it was a minor problem ... I don't remember the name ... these medical terms are so difficult ... blood clot or something ... anyway a small operation fixed the problem and she was feeling better right after the operation."

"I wish we had basic medical facilities in our town, Ma," said Jacob fervently. "I cannot bear to see our people suffering so badly because of corruption."

"God knows what is best. We don't fall sick without His knowledge," said Ma anticipating a difficult conversation.

The church service was a very pleasant affair. Jacob walked with Ma and Edwin and they sat on the same pew with Rosie and her mother. Jacob drowned his doubts in the beautiful music. The sermon was based on Matthew 26:52. '... for all they that take the sword shall perish with the sword.' The pastor spoke eloquently about shunning violence and accepting worldly authorities as ordained by God.

"That is only half the story. What about the leaders? What about their corruption? What about the injustice and the atrocities?" questioned Jacob inwardly.

After the service as they thronged the narrow gate, one of the church elders, Elder Chen, came up to them and touched Jacob's arm.

"Good to see you, son," he said. "We miss you at Sunday school."

"Sorry, I don't seem to have enough time anymore," replied Jacob trying to be polite. "I have been too busy these days."

"Sunday is the Lord's day. You must not do any kind of work on Sunday. You must devote the entire day to worship."

"Yes, I agree. But practically there are so many things for which there is not enough time during weekdays ..." said Jacob lamely.

"I will pray that you will be again as active in church as you were before," said Elder Chen. Then he added after a brief pause, "At least I'm glad that you are not involved in the rebellion and violence that is sweeping our once peaceful land."

"There is some justification for their demands. They are fighting against injustice," said Jacob.

"Don't give me that liberation theology stuff!" admonished Elder Chen. "It is all un-Christian. You know our church does not teach that kind of new-fangled liberation theology."

Jacob was tempted to defend his position but then realized that arguing with Elder Chen was futile. Elder Chen always stoutly defended the canons of the church and condemned all other points of view as heretical. There was nothing to be gained from explaining his view of the conflict. The last thing he wanted was to jeopardize his secret role or give the impression that he was an active sympathizer.

As the crowd inched forward to the gate, Jacob looked around for Rosie. In the mass of people, she was nowhere to be seen.

"I must talk to her today," Jacob told himself. "I must strike while the iron is hot."

When they reached home, Jacob noticed a small piece of yellow paper stuck to the lintel of the front door. Ma noticed it too and wondered how it had got there.

"The wind must have blown it there," said Jacob reaching up to take it down. But he knew what it meant. The emissary from the SNLF must have come in his absence. He could barely control his impatience as his mother prepared tea. Then he was out striding towards the town not knowing where he would meet the messenger on a Sunday when all the shops were closed. He didn't have to go far. There was the young man in the black leather jacket sitting on the culvert at the first bend in the main road. He was the same young man who had come the previous time.

"It's you again," said Jacob slowing down to stop.

"Yes, it's me," replied the man standing up and brushing the dust off his jeans.

"I thought we had agreed not meet on Sundays," said Jacob.

"I know. This is an emergency. The Chief Commander wanted me to bring you the message today itself."

"OK. If it is an emergency, it's all right. What is the problem?"

"The first thing is money. We need a second funding. We need another two hundred thousand. I know you won't have it today. I will take it from you in the parking lot opposite the bank tomorrow morning."

"That is easily arranged," said Jacob relaxing.

"Actually, there is more. We need to talk. Let's get out of the town. Is that alright?"

"How long will it take?" asked Jacob.

"Not too long. Maybe an hour."

The messenger pulled out a cell phone and whispered something unintelligible.

"Just calling up the jeep," he explained. "It should be here in a few minutes."

They kept walking at a leisurely pace. Jacob had a vague foreboding that something significant was afoot and an irreversible decision would soon have to be made.

The covered nondescript jeep soon arrived. As they sped out of town Jacob realized that the outward appearance was deceptive and the jeep was in perfect condition, even possibly new. When Jacob inquired, the messenger confirmed, "Yes, the chassis and the engine are new. We put it under an old body as a camouflage."

Soon they were outside the town and on both sides lay green paddy fields. The messenger gave a short command and the driver pulled the vehicle to the shoulder and stopped. The driver then got out and walked ahead along the side of the road.

The messenger waited till the driver was out of earshot. Then he turned to Jacob and, holding out his hand, said simply, "My name is Thanga". After a brief pause he added modestly, "Actually, General Thanga."

Jacob shook the General's hand and replied, "I am honored to know that you are a General. You already know my name." Then he added with a smile, "You don't look old enough to be a General!"

"I will take that as a compliment. The average age in our army is twenty-nine. It is not like the federal army which is full of pot-bellied, lily-livered middle-aged men."

"I admire the SNLF. You all are the heroes of our tribe," said Jacob.

"Thank you. It is an unequal war and we need to fight with all our strength and cunning to beat the occupiers. They have so much more resources – armored cars, modern machine guns, comfortable tents, rations, and excellent medical care. Even an air force that they will not hesitate to use to bomb us into submission. We have nothing except the love of our land to keep us going."

"Yes, it is that fierce love that drives me too."

"You are doing wonderful work. That is why we are having this meeting," said General Thanga.

"I'm flattered. I don't think I have done anything really outstanding. But I have this great urge to do something extraordinary for our people," said Jacob.

"No, you are being unnecessarily modest. You are a wonderful fundraiser and you keep the accounts so accurately. We have heard nothing but praise from Sau Philipson about your commitment and your trustworthiness."

"No sacrifice of mine can be adequate for our land. I am willing to make the ultimate sacrifice, if necessary. But I don't believe in suicide bombings," said Jacob.

"We heard about your desire to assassinate the police chief."

"Who? The DGP Jasbir?" asked Jacob in surprise. "How did you know that?"

"Yes, the Director General of Police. We are in constant touch with Sau Philipson and several others to ensure our victory."

That was something Jacob already knew but he really wanted to do this on his own. He was disappointed that Philipson hadn't kept his confidence.

"I want to teach him – and the other occupiers – a lesson. A lesson they will not easily forget. I cannot wait for eternity to see justice done. I want to mete

96

it out now as payment for all the wrongs they have done to our people. And I want to strike fear into the deepest corners of their heart."

"It is a very risky venture. You know that. He is the most closely guarded person – even more than Chief Minister Sau Chapang. You have no experience in all this. If you fail you will be killed."

"There is also an equal chance that I will not fail. As I already told you, I am willing to lay down my life for our cause. It might inspire other young men to do the same."

"Looks like you have made up your mind. What support would you need from our side?" asked General Thanga.

"I need three of your best soldiers in federal army uniforms," said Jacob.

"That is easily arranged. We have plenty of our enemy's uniform in all kinds of sizes. But is that all?"

"No, all three must be armed with standard issue automatic pistols. At least one of them must be an excellent marksman. Their automatics must be fitted with silencers."

"We train our boys very well. They can hit a matchbox from two hundred feet."

"That's good. It won't be that far, though," Jacob said with a smile.

"Anything else?" asked General Thanga.

"Yes, at least one of them must be fluent in *Dindi*, the national language that we all totally detest. And one last thing – a captain's uniform for myself with all the decorations and ribbons," said Jacob.

"That can be arranged too. But how do you plan to do this?"

"It is still just an idea in my head. And I want to make it foolproof. I want to think through all the possible obstacles first. It may be best if I just did this on my own. That way if I failed, you can honestly deny any involvement," said Jacob.

"I don't think so. You forget that the lives of three of our soldiers will also be at stake. We need to know. You have no experience in this line of work," said General Thanga with a hint of annoyance.

"I will not play with the lives of our soldiers. I will not be rash." And then Jacob added with a trace of resignation, "All right, if you insist, I will tell you the plan beforehand. There are a few more loose ends to tie up."

"Very well. If you pull this off successfully it will be the biggest act of retaliation so far. It will be a slap in the face of the federal government and a deep embarrassment to the puppet provincial government."

"I know. And that is my plan," said Jacob unsmilingly.

"You know, we need more men and women to join the SNLF. Our recruits are mostly rural youth with no education. We need some educated urban members too."

"I know that it is easier to recruit in the villages than in the towns. What can you expect with a real unemployment rate of eighty-seven per cent although the government officially pegs it at just nine percent?" said Jacob.

"What about you? Why don't you join us? You are physically fit."

"I have thought about it. It is not that I don't want to join. The life of the jungle – sleeping in the open and eating snakes and crows doesn't bother me. I have my widowed mother and younger brother to take care of. My mother is so pious, she will be heartbroken if she came to know that I joined the anti-government forces."

"What about killing the DGP?" asked General Thanga.

"That will be my contribution to our struggle – big enough to compensate for my not enlisting. My mother will know only if I fail."

"Fair enough. Don't botch it. We cannot afford to lose four lives."

"I will plan it well and hope nothing unexpected comes up," said Jacob.

"Right. About the money, can we meet in the parking lot of the bank tomorrow at ten o'clock?" asked General Thanga.

"Yes, I will have the money ready."

With that, the meeting was over. General Thanga clapped his hands together and the driver who was standing at a fair distance came on the double. They rode in silence and after dropping Jacob off near the center of town the jeep sped away on the empty Sunday road.

\*\*\*

The next day Jacob called Rosie on her cell phone.

"Were you sleeping? I am sorry."

"That's OK. I was just taking a nap. What's up?" asked Rosie sleepily.

"Can you meet me at the cathedral in thirty minutes. There's something I want to discuss with you. It is important."

"I will be there."

Jacob walked to the cathedral in the mellow warmth of the afternoon sun enjoying the beauty of the small, well-maintained flower gardens in front of houses and the blue, forest-covered mountains in the far distance.

As he waited for Rosie in the front of the cathedral he got a call from Philipson and a short while later Ben drove up to the steps of the cathedral and delivered an envelope. Without opening it Jacob knew what it was – the authorization for tomorrow's payment and the piece of currency for identification.

Rosie came shortly after, her puffy eyes evidence of having just woken from sleep.

"Good afternoon, sleeping beauty!" said Jacob smiling.

"Whatever it is, it had better be important. I was in the middle of the best siesta in months when you woke me up," pouted Rosie.

"I need the Commandant's jeep," said Jacob matter-of-factly.

"Where do you want to go? I will have to talk to the driver or the adjutant," said Rosie.

"No, I won't need the driver – just the jeep," said Jacob bluntly.

"What? Are you crazy? What do you want me to do? Steal the colonel's jeep in his absence?" said Rosie, now wide-awake, her voice rising in pitch.

"I want it for just thirty minutes. Maximum. Maybe, even less. Is there any way you can beg, borrow or steal it?"

"I don't know how I will do it. That's impossible! What do you need it for anyway?" asked Rosie skeptically.

"You are the only one I can tell this to because I trust you. I need the colonel's jeep to kill Jasbir the DGP."

"Have you lost your senses? Are you out of your mind?" exclaimed Rosie her eyes widening in alarm.

"No. But I want to repay him for the atrocities he has done to us, especially our women. And I want to see with my own eyes the fear in his eyes before he is killed without mercy."

Rosie looked at him wordlessly as if she was seeing him for the first time. Finally, she said, "I don't believe this. You have avoided violence all your life. Now you want to kill? I fear for your life. The DGP is well protected. If they kill you, my life is over," said Rosie softly.

Jacob reached out to brush back a lock of hair from her forehead. "There's a risk in everything we do. Bigger goals have bigger risks. I won't be doing this on my own. I will be there but I am really only the strategist. Now will you get me that jeep?" he asked gently.

"I will try," she said with a resolve that surprised even her, though she had no idea then how she would do it.

"Thank you, Rosie. I always knew I could depend on you. If there is anyone who can do the impossible, it is you. Will you come to my house for dinner? Ma will be very happy."

"Sorry, Jacob. I have to go home. Mother is not well."

After a few steps, she turned around and looked at him with her head cocked to the right.

"Remember what you told me about our army needing new volunteers?" she asked.

"Yes. As a matter of fact, the request has been repeated again. They are in dire need of additional hands," said Jacob.

"I am seriously thinking of signing up," she said, her eyes intently searching his for his reaction.

It was what she expected. He realized she was serious and his mouth opened in wordless surprise.

"And you know what? Whatever it is that you are planning, I think you will succeed," she said. You think differently from others. And there is nothing you cannot do. I always knew that. That's what attracted me to you. You are a real Strelnikov, Jacob."

***

Jacob went home and spent the better part of the night writing a proposal for a grant of ten thousand katas from the police department for holding an anti-insurgent day- camp for high school students.

## Chapter 10

Early next morning Jacob went to Jaya Electronics and under the pretext of updating the shop's accounts quickly typed up the grant proposal he had written the previous night. He added a suitably worded cover letter praising the work the police department was doing and the sacrifices they were making in the fight against misguided youth who joined the underground army.

"I am happy you have come so early in the morning," said Rajesh.

"I knew I would find you here this early. It makes good business sense to be the first to open in the morning. You can sell more," said Jacob smiling.

From the shop, Jacob went to the bank and withdrew two hundred thousand katas in five hundred kata bills. He stuffed the four bundles into his jacket pocket and walked briskly over to the parking lot. General Thanga was waiting, looking more like a serious young man than the guerilla fighter that he was. The formalities were quickly completed and the money changed hands.

"You have any further details you want to share?" asked General Thanga with a searching look.

"I am going into the lion's den," said Jacob cryptically.

"You need to keep in touch with us. Here's a cell phone number to call. A woman will answer your call and she will patch us together through a radio relay."

"How do I identify myself?" asked Jacob.

"Say you are Daniel," said the General with a faint smile.

***

The security was tight at the Police Headquarters. Jacob's heart sank. This was going to be more difficult than he had thought. He was frisked after passing through a metal detector and was then taken to a sergeant who asked him in a bored voice why he wanted to see the Director General while simultaneously scanning through the three-page proposal that he had placed in a clear plastic folder. While he was waiting, he watched an army major and four non-commissioned officers being waved through security exactly as he had seen it happen some weeks earlier when he had been there on an errand for Philipson. "Little has changed. The chink in the armor I was hoping for is still there!" he exulted inwardly. The sergeant made a call on the internal telephone but swiveled around in his chair and lowered his voice so Jacob would not hear what was being said. He had to wait another thirty-five minutes in the dismal room before he was cleared to meet the Director General of Police. A policeman led him from the sergeant's room up a flight of stairs and down a long passage to the office of the Adjutant to the Director General. Jacob was careful to make mental notes of the location of the doors and windows that he passed on the way from the front sergeant's room to the Director General's. He had expected to pass through a maze of rooms staffed with innumerable uniformed policemen but was surprised to find that the Director General's office was in a secluded wing away from the rest of the office. The other officers, Jacob noticed, had their desks in a large hall in the left wing while the Director General's office was at the far end of the right wing, past a string of closed doors on either side of the corridor. The right wing was isolated and eerily quiet. "This is only to be expected considering the nefarious activities of the DGP," thought Jacob. He did not have to wait long in the Adjutant's room. The major and the junior officers came out in a short while and it was his turn. The Director General was smoking a cigar and reading papers in a yellow folder. When he saw Jacob enter the room, he quickly pushed the papers under other folders on the table.

"Sit down, sit down," said the DGP waving the hand that held the cigar.

"Thank you, sir," said Jacob.

"Now what can I do for you, young man?" asked the DGP in an artificially jovial vein.

Jacob thought Jasbir was decidedly ugly. His thick, lecherous lips and dyed and pomaded hair gave him the look of a jaded and unscrupulous debauchee.

"I would like to organize a youth camp to reverse the trend of our young people joining the underground army. The aim is to keep them in the mainstream of society and prevent them from drifting away into violent anti-national activities," said Jacob mouthing the inane phrases that politicians generally used.

"The underground is not an army. They are a bunch of petty terrorists. But your idea is good. It will be good PR for the police and the government. How much will it cost?" asked the DGP already distracted by something else.

"I would like to show the softer side of the police. The aim is to show the police force as friendly and responsive. The police must be seen as the protectors of the rights of ordinary people. This will increase the trust of the public," said Jacob managing to keep a straight face.

"Yes, that is all very good," said the DGP impatiently. "But how much will it cost?"

"I am requesting ten thousand katas, sir," said Jacob.

The DGP looked at him without a word. He seemed to be sizing him up.

"Young man, you need to learn how to do business. You asked for ten thousand. I will give you twenty thousand. Change your request to include activities and expenses of the police participation in the youth camp. We have our own expenses you know. When do you want to do this?"

"After a month, sir."

"These things should be done quickly. Do not waste time waiting. Revise your proposal and give it to the sergeant at the reception. He will ask you to come and collect a check for twenty thousand. After you get the money from the bank, come back and pay my Adjutant the police department's share of ten thousand."

"Yes, sir," said Jacob with what he hoped was an adequately conspiratorial look.

Inside he was thinking, "You thieving, cruel bastard! If I have my way you will never live to get that ten thousand."

"Anything else?" asked the DGP tapping a paperweight on the glass top of the table and Jacob realized that the interview was over.

"Thank you, sir, for the approval," said Jacob and quickly turned and walked, on purpose, towards the wrong door. He had barely opened the door that led directly to the outside corridor when the DGP shouted and waved him to the other door through which he had come in. He muttered a hasty apology and stepped into the Adjutant's chamber again. But the Adjutant was on the phone and merely pointed to the door. As he stepped out of the office he began counting the number of steps to the front reception and re-confirming the position of doors and windows along the passageway.

When he was outside in the open air, he breathed a huge sigh of relief. He said to himself, "Security in the hands of the illiterate and the uneducated is no security at all. The weakest link was always the front end. Security arrangements may have the outward show of being thorough but to the astute observer there were always holes the size of an elephant."

He suddenly had a gut feeling it could be pulled off. It all depended on putting the other pieces together. But there was no time to be lost. If it had to be done, it had to be done now. Jacob felt as if it was a once-in-a-lifetime aligning of the planets. It was now or never. He realized intuitively that the absence of Colonel Kattar was critical to the success of the mission.

The crucial part was getting the Commandant's jeep. It all depended on Rosie talking the army adjutant into lending her the jeep. If it did not work, he would have to get another jeep spruced up to resemble the Commandant's and that was not going to be easy.

"Fortune favors the brave," Jacob decided and went home. Ma's cooking never tasted better. He asked for so many extra helpings of rice, lentils, and beef that his brother Edwin looked at him quizzically over the top of his plate that he balanced in the palm of his left hand. Jacob washed his hands in the aluminum bowl and then announced, "I'm going to lie down for some time."

The fullness of the belly and the aftermath of the adrenaline-rush of visiting the police HQ combined to bring on slumber almost immediately.

\*\*\*

When he awoke, it was mid-afternoon. He turned over on his back and stared at the canvas ceiling that covered the rusty tin roof. "It will have to be done in the next few days," he reminded himself as he swung his legs over the side of the bed.

"What if I botched it? What if my calculations went wrong? What if something unexpected popped up and upset my plans?" he asked himself.

"I'd be dead," he acknowledged somberly.

That sobering thought changed his perception as he walked into the kitchen. Looking at Ma crouched over the fire on the low bamboo stool, Jacob felt a twinge of remorse. "Why am I subjecting my God-fearing, widowed mother to all this pain? How tragic would my death be to her? And the shame of her son turning out to be a violent terrorist and anarchist!"

Jacob needed fresh air. He slipped out to the garden and looked at the plants and the pomegranate and magnolia trees in the backyard. If he failed, he would never see the blue sky and the fluffy white clouds again. "I cannot afford to get sentimental. What needs to be done must be done. I am not prepared to give up, having come this far."

After a quick evening tea with his mother (Edwin was out playing) Jacob hurried off to Jaya Electronics. He reviewed the accounts carefully and reconciled the bank accounts. He debated whether to run the printouts in the store and decided not to. Instead, he transferred the reports to a flash drive, worked on the Warbari's accounts for some time more and then left for the Ace Computer Training School, where he printed out the reports with the accounts and the bank balances.

Then Jacob decided to go unannounced to the house of Philipson.

When he reached the high-walled bungalow, the iron gates remained closed till he rang the bell for the fifth time. He knew that the guards inside were watching him on CCTV cameras before they would let him in. Finally, the gate creaked open.

"Good evening, sir," said the guard respectfully.

"Good evening! Is Sau Philipson in?" asked Jacob.

"The boss is sleeping," said the guard.

"That's all right. I will wait in the sitting room. What about Sau Ben? Is he here?"

"No, sir. Sau Ben left an hour ago with the car on some errand. He will be back only later in the night."

The sitting room was arranged exactly the same way he had seen it at the last meeting. The maids that Philipson employed always kept the room spotlessly clean. The maid who opened the door came back with tea and crackers and the ubiquitous *kuwa* (areca nut and betel leaf). Jacob thumbed through the latest issue of Time as he sipped the tea. When he read the story of how the canine team solved a murder in rural America a thought struck him. The army here had a canine team too. He realized he would need to factor this into his plans.

Philipson walked into the room about forty minutes later yawning and rubbing his eyes. He was barefoot and in t-shirt and jeans.

"What is it, Sau Jacob? Something important?" asked Philipson without any preliminaries.

"I have brought the accounts," said Jacob.

"What is so urgent about that? You know I trust you with the accounts. Why didn't you call me on the phone before coming?" Philipson seemed slightly annoyed.

"I didn't mean to disturb you. I thought it would be good to go over the accounts privately together," said Jacob taking out the reports from the inside pocket of the jacket.

The thought of money appeared to have mollified Philipson a little as he sat down on the sofa to the left of Jacob and held out his hand. It was just as Jacob had suspected. Philipson had no clue what he was looking at as he frowned at the balance sheet that was at the top. He laid that sheet in his lap and looked at the next, which was a list of receipts and payments. The furrowed forehead was evidence that he did not understand this either. He quickly shuffled through the rest and then turned to Jacob.

"Just tell me how much money we have."

Jacob held out his hand for the papers and then pointed to the bank balance figure on the balance sheet.

"That is lower than I expected," said Philipson.

"You must remember I paid two hundred thousand today," said Jacob.

"Ah! I had forgotten that. How are the collections?"

"Nothing yesterday or today. But I think we will get some next week."

"I don't have any to give you today but maybe next week after the weekend. When I meet government officers and rich businessmen at the Evening Club over the weekend, I'll do the usual arm-twisting again."

"I didn't know you went to EC," said Jacob in surprise.

"If I didn't meet them there where else would I meet them? Our town is so small, that is the only common meeting point."

"Keep these statements with you for the record. The last set I gave you was more than a month ago."

"I don't know why we need these statements and reports. I told you I trust you," said Philipson.

"It is not a matter of trust or no trust. We need to have checks and balances. It is always good to keep a set of backup records."

"OK, I will keep this with the last set you gave. What other news? I hope you have given up your foolhardy plan?"

"No, I haven't given it up. But it is something I cannot do on my own. I'm still planning."

"It may be best if you handed your plan over to the SNLF. They are trained to do things like this. You can provide backup support by keeping accounts and helping us with the strategy."

Jacob shrewdly inferred that General Thanga had not divulged their discussions to Philipson.

"I will think about it," said Jacob noncommittally.

When he was outside the house he walked briskly to the main road and then caught a nearly full share-taxi to the Secretariat. From there it was only a short walk to the police headquarters. As he looked at the imposing building and the heavily guarded gate, he faltered momentarily. Then chiding himself for his weakness he pushed thoughts of failure aside and flagged down a taxi.

"I'll take the whole taxi. Don't stop for any more passengers."

"OK. Where do you want to go?"

"Take me to the new bridge below the town," said Jacob as he got into the back seat and pulled the door shut.

As the driver weaved through the mass of pedestrians milling around the government offices, Jacob timed the ride. Once past the government offices, there were fewer impediments. When the taxi finally pulled up near the bridge, Jacob checked his watch. It had taken all of fourteen minutes.

"Shall I wait for you, Sau?" the taxi driver called out as Jacob crossed the road towards the bridge.

"Yes. Give me ten minutes," Jacob called out. He knew the taxi would not get any return passengers to the town at this time of the day.

He looked down from the bridge. As the sunlight danced on the pebbles the water ran clear on the streambed. The water was barely knee-deep at this time of the year. He walked to the other side and looked at the embankments. Both embankments were easy to navigate. He walked further up the road on the other side. There were a shed and a large haystack and a farmhouse some distance further up the road.

He walked leisurely back to the waiting taxi and returned to the Secretariat area.

"That will be eighty katas, Sau," the driver said.

"Here's ninety." Jacob was in a magnanimous mood. It was not the custom in this town to tip taxi drivers.

From there Jacob took a share-taxi home. It was too early for supper. He picked up Guevara's Guerilla Warfare to continue where he had left off.

The cell phone rang. It was one of the collectors.

"I have some bad news. Somebody else has been collecting contributions in our name."

"Have they been handing out receipts?" asked Jacob.

"Yes. I insisted that they show me the receipt. It looks like an exact replica of ours."

"Don't worry. We will set a trap to catch the culprit."

## Chapter 11

While all this was happening, Rosie was at the officers' club in the cantonment. She had not slept a wink the previous night as she agonized over ways to accomplish the task. Whatever the cost, she had to somehow get that jeep for Jacob. She knew she would have to use all her wiles to succeed and failure was not an option. She tossed and turned as she tried to banish the thoughts that came to her mind.

The adjutant was delighted when she called him to tell she was going to be at the club that evening. She was dressed to kill in the tightest jeans she had (a skirt was too risky, she thought) and a red tank top with a plunging neckline. She made it a point to wear the necklace that Colonel Kattar had presented her. She also liberally applied the most alluring perfume she had.

As she sat on the high stool next to the adjutant, the junior officers (second lieutenants and lieutenants) emboldened by the absence of their commanding officer attempted to banter with her.

"When is the Commandant coming back?" she asked the adjutant, Major Rakhod.

"Not feeling lonely, are you Miss?" called out one of the junior officers and the group burst into raucous laughter.

"I'm always at your service. Just call!" shouted another.

The laughter redoubled much to the discomfiture of the adjutant who was unsure of his ability to control the rowdy group of which he was a member when the Commandant was in station. Rosie herself was unfazed by the attention. As a matter of fact, she gave the impression that she was enjoying it.

"Don't mind my colleagues. They are harmless. It is just that they have not been allowed any leave for some months now," explained Major Rakhod.

"Don't worry about it. It doesn't bother me. They are just having fun," said Rosie.

"We could go to another room?" suggested Major Rakhod.

Rosie quickly realized that the adjutant was more vulnerable in the presence of his fellow officers and declined the offer.

"I am comfortable here. This club is nice. Moreover, I cannot stay too long today."

"That's a pity. Stay as long as you can. I will have you dropped home in the Commandant's jeep. At least have dinner before you go," pleaded the adjutant.

"That's very kind of you. I will take you up on that another day." She added thoughtfully after a pause, "Maybe very soon. I have to leave soon today but I really would like to spend some time with you when you have the time."

"That would be lovely." He did not know what else to say as he fidgeted in nervous excitement. As he looked at her tongue-tied, the junior officers tittered amongst themselves.

"I will need the Commandant's jeep for an hour or so. The Commandant told me I could ask you when I needed it."

"Yes, yes. Of course, just let me know and I will send the jeep over." The adjutant was eager to please.

"Thank you, Major! You are so helpful. I am sorry but I must be going. Thank you for the evening, Major Rakhod," said Rosie with a smile.

As they waited outside for the Commandant's jeep, Rosie took a deep breath and made up her mind.

When they were outside the camp area and on the outskirts of the town, Rosie motioned the driver to pull over to the side. The driver was puzzled and looked at her twice to make sure he understood her correctly. When the vehicle came to a standstill, the driver turned to look at her, one hand on the wheel and the other on the gear shift-stick.

Mustering her knowledge of the *Dindi* language, she asked familiarly, "What is your name?"

The driver suddenly seemed to have been overcome by a bout of bashfulness. Gone were the lecherous looks he used to give her as he dropped her off after her meetings with the colonel. He shifted in his seat as he replied respectfully, "My name is Mohan, madam."

"Don't call me madam, Mohan, you know my name."

When she touched his forearm lightly he flinched in confusion. She saw that her attention was having the desired results and she decided to force the issue without further ado.

"Mohan, how would you like to sleep with me?" asked Rosie looking him straight in the eye.

Mohan looked at her in total bewilderment and then looked down at his hands that had dropped to his lap. No words came to his mouth as he sat stunned, wringing his hands.

"Don't be scared, Mohan. I am not joking. You are a strong man and you have been in camp for more than a year. It will be our little secret. No one will know. Look at me." When he hesitatingly turned to look at her, she asked him, "Do you want me or not?"

"Yes, ma'am," he croaked.

"Good. What will you give me in return, Mohan?"

His courage seemed to have returned. "What can I give you ma'am? I have nothing. I am only a poor driver."

"You have many things to give, Mohan," said Rosie gently stroking his hairy forearm. "This jeep, for example."

"This jeep? How can I give you this jeep, ma'am? It is the Commandant's."

"But the Commandant is not here. You know he has allowed me to use his jeep. I don't want it forever. Only for an hour or two."

The driver relaxed visibly. "I can drive you anywhere you want."

"No, I may want only the jeep. If you are willing to ..." she paused as she struggled to find the right word in *Dindi*, "... lend me the jeep – only lend – the jeep for two hours, that would be enough."

"Will I get the jeep back in the same condition? Without any damage?" asked Mohan.

"Of course, you will get it back in exactly the same condition. We will keep it a secret. Our second secret."

Confidence slowly returned to Mohan. He smiled. "This is going to be easy. I cannot believe my luck!" he told himself.

"Please don't tell the Commandant or adjutant about the jeep," Mohan pleaded.

"I already told you, only the two of us will know." Then, reverting to her normal demeanor, she said, "Now I must get home."

As she got down from the jeep in front of her house she whispered softly, "It will be in the next few days. Be ready."

Her mother was sitting by the fireplace sipping tea.

"Ma, I told you not to strain yourself. You must stay in bed. You should not be cooking," said Rosie.

"I am feeling much better. Cooking is not so difficult. If I lie in bed all the time my strength will not come back to me," said Rosie's mother.

"Ma, there is something I must tell you. I need to go away for a few days on some important work. You will have to stay with your sister till I come back."

"I don't want to trouble her. She has her own children. I don't want there to be any misunderstanding between us like the last time. I will stay alone here. I will be all right."

"No, Ma. In that case, I will not go." Then she had an inspiration. "Ma, would you be willing to stay with Nau Hilda, Jacob's mother?"

"She is a saint. I will be happy to stay with her – if she has space in her house for me."

"I think Nau Hilda will be happy if you stayed with her. She always asks me about you when I visit Jacob's house. She is worried that you have not gone back to work yet."

Rosie felt dread and exhilaration at the same time. Things seemed to be falling into place. She knew she could still abort the whole plan but she saw this as her big chance to contribute to the freedom struggle.

She reached for her cell phone to call Jacob.

"The eagle will land. It is ready," she said.

"What! I don't believe it! You mean the real one?" blurted out Jacob in surprise and disbelief.

"Yes, the real one – the one and only. The exact one that you wanted," confirmed Rosie.

"How did you manage to arrange it?" Jacob still did not seem ready to believe.

"Don't worry about the 'how' part. That is my concern. Just let me know when you need it," said Rosie.

"You are amazing! You mean, I can get it whenever I want?"

"Yes, anytime before the colonel gets back. I can get it for you tomorrow if you need it."

"No tomorrow will be too tight. The earliest I can use it is the day after."

"Not a problem. Just let me know."

"I owe you a big favor, Rosie. Many thanks!"

"You don't owe me anything. For one thing, you can't repay this debt. For another, I am doing it for my land and my people."

"I am grateful," said Jacob softly. "I will call and confirm the date."

"Please do."

"Just let me know if there is anything at all I can do," added Jacob.

"Actually, there is something. Can I have my mother stay at your place for a few days till we finish this job? She and your mother are the best of friends."

"Sure! That will be no problem. In fact, it would make Ma very happy to have the company of your mother."

"Thanks! I will bring her over tomorrow if you set the date for the day after," Rosie said ending the call.

When she went to the kitchen again to speak to her mother, she felt an indescribable sadness looking at her frail mother crouched on the low bamboo stool staring out of the open kitchen door. She knew that the decision she had taken would break her mother's heart if she ever came to know of it. The values her mother had instilled in her wrestled with the love for her tribe and the intense hatred she felt towards the alien occupiers.

"Ma, I will pack your things for tomorrow. I just spoke to Jacob. He said Nau Hilda would be very happy to have you stay with her."

"When are you taking me there?"

"Most probably tomorrow afternoon, Ma."

"And where are you going?"

"Not far, Ma. I will tell you when I come back."

When she went back to the bedroom to pack she realized that her coming back was indefinite. In fact, she may never come back. One could never be certain in battle. She pushed thoughts of death aside and began to pack. All she needed for herself fit in a small bag. There was just a second change of clothes and a small bag of toiletries; no perfumes, no extra shoes, nothing fancy. The stylish earrings, the elegant necklaces, and the chic bracelets, she left behind in her trunk. The one ornament that she chose to carry was the gold chain that the Commandant, Colonel Kattar, had given her and for which she had paid him a token price. The irony of selecting her enemy's gift was not lost on her and she smiled wryly as she hung it around her neck for the second time that day. She was in the middle of packing her mother's clothes when Jacob called back.

"Rosie, I have decided to set the time for 10:30 a.m. on Wednesday, the day after tomorrow. I just spoke to our HQ."

"Isn't that too early in the day? You know how our government officers are. No one comes in before noon," said Rosie.

"Yes, I know. They act as if they are kings, these shameless bureaucrats of ours. They set such a terrible example for their subordinates in the civil service. But you forget that it is only our own flesh and blood that act like this. To their credit, the alien occupiers have a higher sense of punctuality. Our person of interest comes into work at ten o'clock sharp every day."

"I see. But in that case, shouldn't the time be ten or even nine fifty-five, just as he comes in to work?" asked Rosie.

"You mean, hit him when he arrives? He is too well protected on the road. I have other plans for him."

"I don't know. Isn't it more risky?" Rosie sounded doubtful. "So, the time is set for 10:30?"

"Yes, that is the best time. The deed would have been done before the government machinery starts the day. They will not know what hit them."

"OK. That's a good strategy. Tell me how much money should I give you for my mother?"

"Are you serious? Don't make me angry. We are in this together. And our mothers are the best of friends. She can stay with us for as long as she likes. All that we have is yours also."

"That's very kind of you to say so, Jacob," said Rosie from the heart.

Immediately after Jacob had hung up, she called Philipson and told him she was signing up for the SNLF. She insisted that she be transferred to the jungle camp on Wednesday.

"I want to be out of the town before noon," she insisted.

Philipson did not argue.

"I have no one else signed up for this week so we will have to send you alone."

"That's no problem. I don't mind traveling alone. I know the SNLF takes good care of its women cadre."

She then sat down and wrote a letter to Jacob.

***

Jacob had, in the meantime, spoken to General Thanga via the cell phone and radio patch identifying himself as Daniel to the woman intermediary. The General confirmed that the men and uniforms and the arms and ammunition would be arriving, as per Jacob's request, in the wee hours of the morning on Wednesday. Jacob suggested that they park their jeep behind the farm shed and haystack just outside the new bridge to the south of the town. General Thanga pressed for more information on the operation and Jacob reluctantly told him it would be carried out in the office. The General's response was, "I am not sure how you can pull that off. I hope you know what you are doing. I don't want to send my men on a suicide mission."

Jacob assured him that if the variables changed unexpectedly, he was prepared to call it off.

When Jacob turned in for the night there remained less than thirty-six hours for the mission to be accomplished. He lay down on the bed but sleep would not come. In his mind, he acted and reenacted the scenario over and over again. He knew the success of the mission depended, to a great extent, on getting the Commandant's jeep. If, for some reason, the jeep did not materialize, the risk would be increased manyfold and has was prepared to call off the mission.

He was not the only one yearning for sleep. Rosie tossed and turned, agonizing over the sacrifice that she had decided to make and how that would irrevocably alter life as she had known it so far.

## Chapter 12

Tuesday passed in a trice for both Jacob and Rosie.

When he woke up the thought came to Jacob that this might well be his last full day in this world. Time and again, that thought returned to him throughout the day. If his plan went awry and there was an exchange of fire with the police, he knew he and his comrades did not have any escape. They would be shred into ribbons by machine gun fire from those trigger-happy guards. But to die instantaneously in a hail of gunfire would be a far better fate than being captured alive. He knew that the federal army uniform was only very transient insurance. Once their subterfuge was exposed, there would be no mercy even if they surrendered. Vicious and barbaric torture followed by death in a staged encounter would be their destiny if they were captured alive. They had to succeed at all costs.

But more than his own death, Jacob worried about the repercussions a failed mission would have on the struggle and on his people. Failure would not only set back the Movement but might even completely end it if the administration responded ruthlessly on civilians. He wondered if he was taking on too much and risking everything. He wondered if discretion was the better part of valor and he should call off the operation.

***

While Jacob pondered on the possibility of death, Rosie brooded over life after the event. This would be the last straw that broke their relationship. Even if Jacob would forgive her, she would not be able to forgive herself. There would be no life left for her in this town. The SNLF would be her purgatory. If she survived active combat and malaria she would come back to society redeemed. Rosie decided to spend the entire day with her mother indoors until it was time to take her to Jacob's house.

***

Jacob's cell phone rang just after the morning brunch. He grimaced when he saw that it was from Philipson. "Had he come to know about the plan?" wondered Jacob. If he had, his task had suddenly become more difficult. Jacob had planned for a swift execution with the shortest possible incubation period. He also wanted the least number of people to know of the plan. He had expressly told General Thanga not to divulge the identity of the target to the three hit men that the General would be sending. They would know that only at the very last minute. But Philipson was calling about something else. Jacob was very relieved.

"The crazy fellow Sau Kamat wants to kill the policemen responsible for the custodial death," said Philipson after the usual preliminaries.

"How does he plan to do that? An attack on the station?" asked Jacob.

"No, Sau Kamat plans to kill a few constables when they come to the market to buy groceries or when they are playing cards in the evening in the courtyard of the police station."

"Are they worth the trouble? They are small fry. Killing them won't hurt the government," argued Philipson.

"True. But, nonetheless, it would be a big embarrassment to the rulers," said Jacob.

"When does he want to do it?" asked Jacob.

"He wants to do it this evening," said Philipson.

"This evening? Today?" Jacob was aghast.

"Why, what's the problem?"

"Can you get Sau Kamat to hold back on this one for a few days till I confirm who the guilty policemen are?"

"Do we really need to do that? They are all guilty," said Philipson.

"I agree, in a way they all are. But the extreme punishment of death must only be inflicted on those who really deserve it beyond the shadow of any doubt. We must not kill the innocent. Otherwise what is the difference between us and them?" asked Jacob trying desperately to get Philipson to rein in Kamat.

Jacob knew that if Kamat attacked the police station tonight he might as well kiss his plans goodbye. The government would immediately impose a curfew and raise the alert level. Another opportunity might never come.

"Sau Kamat is accusing me of being soft. I cannot continue to block his plans for revenge for much longer," said Philipson.

"Just this once. This is not a good time. If he wants he can do it next week. Tell him I will give him the names of the guilty," pleaded Jacob.

"All right," conceded Philipson reluctantly. "I will tell him to wait till next week."

"Please ask Sau Kamat to plan it well. The police may be inefficient and unfit physically, but their firepower is much stronger than ours. A frontal assault may not succeed," warned Jacob.

"Subtlety was never his strong suit," said Philipson with a mocking laugh. "What are you doing today and tomorrow?"

The question caught Jacob unawares. "Me? No, nothing much. The usual ... accounts and some writing ... for the papers," he faltered.

"OK. We need to have another meeting soon," said Philipson hanging up.

Jacob breathed a huge sigh of relief. Then he realized that it was almost 10:30. "Just twenty-four hours left for the hour of reckoning," he told himself.

Surprisingly, the butterflies in his stomach seemed to have all disappeared. There was no anxiety or tension anymore. He remembered that there was something he had to buy.

At the best clothes shop in town, he carefully selected the finest red and white *luan* they had. It was expensive, costing four thousand katas. On a sudden inspiration, he decided to buy one more *luan*. The second one was green with gold embroidery and cost four thousand five hundred katas. The shop assistant made as if to unfold the *luans* so Jacob could take a closer look but Jacob waved her to wrap them up. "If it went according to plan these would never be opened and never worn either," thought Jacob.

On the way back, he bought beef and pork from the butcher's and tomatoes and potatoes as well from the grocery shop. Rosie's mother was coming today and Ma would want to cook a special meal for her. From another store, he bought the finest long grain rice they had. He also bought two packets of chocolates for Edwin. It had been a long time since he had bought anything for his younger brother.

"Ma, here are the provisions for tonight's dinner. I know you want to cook a special dinner for Rosie mother."

"You bought everything yourself? I was planning to go to the market," said Ma.

"I wanted to save you the trouble," Jacob said smiling.

"Where is the oil? And the spices?" asked Ma rummaging through the plastic bag.

"I forgot those. You know I know nothing about cooking!"

"Never mind! At least you bought these and saved me the trouble of carrying the heavy stuff. I will go by myself and buy the other small things I need," said Ma taking the items out carefully from the bag and placing them on the floor.

"Ma, I need to go out for some work. I will be back soon," said Jacob rising from the low bamboo stool.

"Have a cup of tea before you go. Do you know what time Rosie and Nau Elsie are coming?"

"I think they will come in the evening before it is dark. By the way, Ma please cook some extra food for four of my friends. They may come for dinner tonight."

After tea with a bowl of rice, Jacob went to Jaya Electronics. The Warbari owner Rajesh was, as usual, busy counting money.

"Where have you been?" Rajesh asked as he entered.

"I have been busy with some other work. But don't worry, I will post all the pending transactions and bring the accounts up-to-date today," replied Jacob.

As the computer booted up Jacob sorted all the vouchers date-wise. The transactions were not that many, as the sales for each day was a consolidated amount. But the complication was that each transaction had to be posted twice, first in the real account books and then in the other tax evasion set of accounts called 'second'.

While updating the accounts of Jaya Electronics, Jacob also surreptitiously entered the transactions of the Movement from a small piece of paper with handwritten coded numbers. Jacob decided to increase the 'emergency fund' buried in the backyard from two hundred thousand to three hundred thousand katas. He needed to draw seventy thousand katas from the bank to top up the thirty thousand he had under the mattress.

While waiting at the bank Jacob had a sudden inspiration. He decided on a lark to go to the Catholic cathedral. As he slowly pulled open the heavy doors of the cathedral and stepped inside he realized he was not alone. There were other heads bowed down in prayer. He sat down in the nearest pew and looked up at the high stained glass windows through which sunlight streamed into the darkened chapel. When his eyes adjusted to the dimness he recognized the figure kneeling at the pew across from the aisle and a few rows ahead. It was Rosie. He moved noiselessly to her pew and sat down next to the kneeling Rosie. But Rosie sensed his presence and looked up, her eyes widening in surprise when she recognized Jacob. After her prayer, she rose up to sit on the pew next to Jacob. Neither of them talked. The cares of the world seemed to have disappeared – there was just peace and quiet.

When they stepped out into the sunlight a short while later, Rosie turned to ask Jacob, "How did you find me here? One of your secret informers?"

"No!" laughed Jacob. "Nothing of the sort. I was at the bank when I got the idea of coming here. Not for prayer – just for some quiet time."

"I came to pray," replied Rosie. "Our Presbyterian church is open only on Sundays. The Catholics keep their churches open all the time."

"Let's not discuss theology. It is good to see you."

"I am happy to see you. There are many things that we need to talk about."

"There are? Like what?" asked Jacob feigning surprise.

"You know what I mean. But this is not a good time. I hope we can go back to being what we were before," said Rosie wistfully.

"I know. We will need a time machine for that. But I hope all this will be over soon and we can return to being just ordinary people leading lives of quiet desperation."

"That day may never come," Rosie said with a sigh.

Jacob realized that that was probably true and he had no comforting words.

As they descended the steps of the cathedral to the main road below, Jacob took Rosie's hand in his.

"I love you, Rosie."

"I love you too, Jacob," said Rosie disengaging her hand to pull out a handkerchief from her handbag to dab at her eyes as they welled with tears.

"Let's go and have some tea before we go home," suggested Jacob.

Rosie readily agreed and they caught a taxi to the Bamboo Grove. Over steaming tea and dumplings they looked at each other but did not articulate their thoughts.

"These dumplings are good, aren't they?" asked Jacob.

"Yes, they are. They are always good."

Later as they stepped out of the restaurant Jacob asked, "What time will you come with your mother?"

"Very soon. In about an hour," replied Rosie.

Then they caught share-taxis and went their separate ways to their homes.

On reaching his house, Jacob took out the thirty thousand from under the mattress and added it to the seventy thousand he had just drawn from the bank. He counted the notes twice to make sure there was a hundred thousand. He then placed them under the mattress again.

Rosie came with her mother an hour and a half later. Ma gave Nau Elsie a warm welcome hugging her and telling her how beautiful she looked. Jacob took the bag from Rosie's hand and carried it into the bedroom.

After tea and an hour of talking, they all had an early meal. Ma had outdone herself. Rosie's mother disregarded doctor's orders and enjoyed the food.

After supper, Jacob walked Rosie to the main road. In the dark, they wordlessly held each other close.

"Good luck tomorrow! Be careful," said Rosie.

"Good luck to you too. Thanks for everything."

When he got home he took the shovel from the shed behind the house and walked to the banana trees where he carefully dug out the two tin boxes. He added the hundred thousand to the box with the money and checked to see if the pistol was intact in the other. It was.

## Chapter 13

The call came at 5:00 a.m. It was brief.

"We are on our way. We should be there by six o'clock."

Jacob had been awake since 4:00 a.m., unable to go back to sleep. He quickly jumped out of bed and went about his morning ablutions after first placing water in an aluminum pot on the kerosene stove to heat for a quick bath. The water was warm by the time he came back and he bathed hurriedly, sloshing the lukewarm water on his body from the plastic bucket in the bathroom. When he came back to the kitchen, Ma was already up, lighting the wood fire.

"Son, where are you going so early?" asked Ma.

"Good morning, Ma, I have some urgent business to do today. My day starts early today," Jacob replied apologetically.

"You have become very mysterious in recent weeks. It is time you started confiding in your mother like you did before," she sighed.

"Someday I will tell you everything, Ma."

"I will be the happiest mother when that day comes."

"Ma, the extra food I asked you to prepare yesterday – can you pack four lunch packets with that? I will only have a cup of tea now. I will eat with my friends later."

In forty minutes Jacob was ready in his blue jeans, white shirt and black leather jacket. He carefully picked up the plastic shopping bag containing the two expensive *luans*. Uncharacteristically, he kissed his mother goodbye and ran to the road, carrying the four banana-leaf wrapped lunches in a plastic bag in one hand and the bag with the *luans* in the other. He knew a taxi would be difficult to find this early in the morning. He hurried towards the center of town, half running. Ten minutes later he spied a taxi in the distance. The driver was on the lookout for passengers leaving for Ultapur on the 6:00 a.m. bus. These passengers were happy to pay a twenty percent premium for the early morning hours. The taxi driver was rather surprised when he mentioned the new bridge below the town, in the opposite direction, as his destination. The ride took exactly nine minutes, a full five minutes less than when he had timed the ride in a taxi earlier, although his part of town was farther away from the bridge than Police Headquarters. He knew that the next time he would drive on this route, traffic would be at its peak. This was the weakest link in his plans. If there was a traffic snarl they may be forced to abandon their vehicle and escape on foot.

He paid the taxi off on the town side of the bridge and the taxi sped back to town in search of early morning travelers to Ultapur. He crossed the bridge and walked up the incline to the haystack and shed. They had not arrived. He sat down on a large stone near the haystack and contemplated the green hills and the sunlight warming up the morning air. He listened to the birds singing in the far distance. Jacob felt a strange sense of calm.

He called Rosie. She was already awake.

"Where are you, Jacob?" she asked.

"I am outside the town at the rendezvous point."

"What are you doing so early? It's not even seven o'clock."

"The team needs to rest after their drive in. And we also need to discuss the plan."

"Jacob, I am scared. If anything happens to you, my life is over," said Rosie with a quaver in her voice.

"Rosie, I feel the same way about you. When all this is over we will have time for each other." Jacob could not prevent his voice from choking.

"Ever the Strelnikov, aren't you? Country first!" she replied without malice or anger.

"Have you called the cantonment yet?" asked Jacob.

"It is way too early. I will call them at the right time. And I will call you when the jeep is here."

About fifteen minutes later he spotted the jeep at the top of the hill and watched it as it played hide and seek coming down the winding roads. The jeep made little sound as the driver had switched off the engine and was coasting downhill. Jacob stood up and signaled the driver to pull the jeep off the road and bring it behind the haystack.

One by one the three stepped out of the vehicle. Jacob had not seen any of them before. The leader walked up to Jacob holding out his hand. He was big and tall but the distinguishing feature was that he could have, at first sight, easily passed for a person of the plains. He did not have the tribal features of the other two. Jacob presumed that he was of mixed parentage. He had not heard of hired mercenaries from outside the Somi tribe.

"We are here for the operation on the orders of the General," the leader said.

"Thank you for coming. We have to wait for a few hours. Hope you won't mind," said Jacob.

"No problem. We are trained to be patient – to wait for the perfect moment."

"Good! I have brought food for you. We will eat first and then we will wait for the call."

"From whom? Our General?" asked the leader of the group.

"No, from my partner. By the way, my name is …"

"It is best if there are no introductions. This is a high-risk job and there is a possibility of being captured alive. It is best if we really did not know all the details. We are doing this together but as soon as this operation is over it is unlikely that we will ever meet."

Jacob considered this for a minute. Then he said, "Makes sense. How shall we address each other?"

"You are the leader for this. So, you are Number 1 or just 1. I am Number 2. He is Number 3 and the other Number 4. We will just go by numbers."

"Good! In another four hours, we should be going our separate ways again."

"So, what is the plan? The modus operandi?" asked Number 2.

"In a short while from now, I will go and get our transport for this job. We will not be using your vehicle. It would be too obvious. Your driver – Number 4? – will drive us to the location. The three of us will enter the office. You will use your *Dindi* skills to tell the guards at the entrance that I am the new major and that on Colonel Kattar's orders you have brought gifts for our target. Number 3 will open the plastic bag to show the presents."

"What are the presents?" asked Number 2.

"Good question!" said Jacob opening the plastic bag to show the red and white and green and gold *luans*.

"My! They are beautiful! Must be very expensive," blurted out Number 3.

"They are. Our target is a womanizer of the worst kind. He has dishonored our women in unspeakable ways. These *luans* will be our passports if we play our cards right."

"And then?" asked Number 2.

"We liquidate our target, make our exit and get back to this very same spot. You will head back to your hideout and I will drive the hit vehicle back to town."

"What makes you think our exit will be so easy?" asked Number 2.

"If everything goes according to plan, it will be."

"And if not?" persisted Number 2.

"We will have to surrender. It is not a good idea to get drawn into a shootout in a crowded office building," said Jacob somberly.

"It is difficult for us to surrender. That is a fate worse than death," replied Number 2 looking Jacob in the eyes.

"Let's hope will all happen as planned. Who is the sharpshooter here?" asked Jacob.

"It is Number 3. But what is the distance?" asked Number 2.

"Close range. Very close range. Maybe four meters. Maximum five."

"In that case, I will do the shooting. Number 3 is best from long distance. He will be the back-up," said Number 2.

"Have you brought along the silencers?"

"Of course, these new ones are good. You hear only a dull thud."

"Good. There is one other thing. The army has a canine squad, a dog team. To throw them off our scent we will wade through the stream when we get back here. We won't use the bridge," said Jacob.

"Got it. I can't wait to kill the guy. Let's have our food first."

There was no water to wash their hands.

"Sorry I forgot," said Jacob apologetically.

"Four, run down to the stream and bring back a jerry can of water," commanded Jacob.

"I am not sure if the water is clean," said Jacob.

"Clean? We are not like you city guys. We drink even from puddles or squeeze leaves for water when there is no water to drink. We live on crows and mice and snakes. Clean water? Who cares!" laughed Number 2 uproariously.

Each unwrapped a banana leaf packet on the ground in front of him and began to eat after saying grace.

"This food is very tasty. I have not had beef and pork for weeks now," said Number 4 who had not said a word till now.

"Thank you, my mother cooked this," said Jacob quietly.

They ate in silence. When they had finished, Number 4 carried the rolled-up leaf wrappings to a clump of grass some distance away. All four washed their hands with water from the jerry can. Then the visitors lifted the jerry can to their mouths and gulped large mouthfuls of water but Jacob politely refused.

After the meal, the three soldiers took out tobacco and rolled cigarettes. Jacob declined the offer. The country tobacco emitted a strong, pungent odor.

"Keeps the insects away," said Number 2 smiling.

"I don't smoke but don't mind me. Go ahead and smoke."

"Not just the insects. Tobacco juice is good protection against leeches. You cannot get away from them in the jungle."

Jacob was a little apprehensive about smoking right next to the haystack but he decided it was wiser to keep quiet. While Number 3 and Number 4 pulled handfuls of hay to fashion makeshift pillows,

Number 2 just leaned against the haystack. Their cigarettes finished, Number 3 and Number 4 were soon asleep. Number 2 took out a small, weather-beaten pad from his pocket and scribbled notes.

The call came at eight thirty. His cell phone was in silent mode and it did not wake the two who were asleep. Number 2 looked at Jacob expectantly but did not say a word.

Jacob walked away from the group and took the call.

"I just called the cantonment. The jeep will be here by nine o'clock," said Rosie.

"Good job!" said Jacob. "I knew I could trust you to get this done."

"Let us not congratulate ourselves just yet. Many things can still go wrong."

"O.K."

"I will call you again and let you know where to pick up the jeep." Then she added, "Whatever happens I love you."

"I love you too. Please don't worry too much. If I find it too risky, I will call it off."

"Please be careful. Forgive me for everything."

"What is there to forgive? I am the one who should ask for forgiveness from you. After all, I am the Strelnikov," said Jacob.

"Never mind all that. Just wait for my call."

Jacob did not know it then but that would be the last time they had a two-way conversation.

***

When Jacob came back to the haystack he spoke to Number 2. "I must go to the town now. Our vehicle will be ready for pick up soon."

Jacob walked across the bridge and walked about a kilometer before he found a taxi headed into town. By the time the two who were asleep woke up, Jacob was in the vacant parking lot of the bank.

*** 

Rosie had a quick shower and arranged everything in the house. She placed the envelope with the letter to Jacob on her mother's bed. And then she waited.

At two minutes to nine, the jeep drew up. She peered out from behind the curtain to see which jeep the driver had brought – it was the Commandant's own. As Mohan stepped out of the jeep she moved to the front door to open it.

"Good morning, ma'am!" Mohan wished her self-consciously.

This time she didn't care about him addressing her as ma'am. Nor did she care about the neighbors seeing the army jeep at her door. Her mind was focused entirely on the task at hand.

"Mohan, where are the keys?"

"Here ma'am. Where is your friend?" Mohan still seemed hesitant about handing over the jeep.

"He is not here. He will come. Just leave the keys in the ignition."

"Ma'am ..." Mohan was about to protest.

"It will be safe. We have no car thieves in our town. And no one will dare touch an army jeep," said Rosie.

"O.K., ma'am," said Mohan and walked back to the jeep to leave the keys.

When he came back the door was ajar and he walked in, latching the door behind him. Rosie was in the middle of the sitting room with her cell phone to her ears. With her left hand, she motioned him to be silent and then spoke curtly into the phone in the Somi language, which she knew Mohan would not understand.

"It is in front of my house. Come and pick it up. I am taking the driver to the bazaar to buy him a few things. Bring it back as soon as you can and leave it exactly where you found it." Then she turned off the phone before Jacob could reply.

Rosie and Mohan looked at each other. She again wished all this was not happening. She felt like excusing herself to go to the bathroom and then jumping out of the window and running away. But she knew if she did that the whole plan would fail. Mohan would run out and get away in his jeep and Jacob would have no way of completing his mission.

"What are you waiting for?" she asked without emotion and Mohan moved like an automaton.

As she surrendered herself a short while later she heard the jeep start and drive off.

***

This was the first time that Jacob had driven a jeep like this one. The powerful engine purred as he drove it towards the bridge. He soon overtook the taxi that had brought him to Rosie's house. Traffic was all headed into town at this time of the morning and he had no trouble driving in the opposite direction. But he drove carefully. The last thing he wanted was to get involved in a crash at this time and that too with the Commandant's jeep. Even with the careful driving, it took him only twelve minutes to get to the haystack.

When he got back to the SNLF soldiers, they looked at him open-mouthed.

"How did you get the Commandant's jeep?" asked Number 2 incredulously.

"I have my contacts," A smiled. "But we need to be careful with it. I want to return it in exactly the same condition."

"How much did you pay for borrowing this? A few million?" joked Number 3.

"Million? I paid nothing!" said Jacob little knowing the price Rosie was paying at that very time.

## Chapter 14

Number 3 ran quickly to the back of the jeep and took out the neatly pressed and starched uniforms.

"Not just yet," said Jacob. "We have another thirty minutes to wait."

Then a doubt struck him. What if the DGP did not come into the office today? The whole effort would be a disastrous failure if they all got arrested, or worse killed, for nothing. He realized that he had overlooked this important aspect in his planning. The presence of the DGP Jasbir had to be confirmed before the attempt was made. He could use the SNLF vehicle to make a quick dash to the town to confirm. But there wasn't time enough for that. It would not only delay the action but also add an element of last minute desperation that he had wanted to avoid. He did not call Rosie as he thought she would be at the bazaar with the driver. He considered calling Philipson for assistance but decided against it. Then he had a sudden brainwave. He decided to call one of his collectors.

"Sau Paul, how are you?" asked Jacob.

"Good morning, Sau Jacob! I am fine. What can I do for you?" Paul sounded delighted to get this call from Jacob.

"How are the collections coming?"

"Not so good. There is someone else collecting in our name. People are unwilling to pay up twice."

"We need to find who those thieves are. But I need your help with something else today," said Jacob.

"Tell me. I am always happy to help."

"Sau Paul, I need to go to the Police Headquarters to find out if they are going to pay any compensation to the mother of the prisoner they killed in custody. But I have other work as well. I want you to watch the entrance of the police HQ and call me when you see the DGP come in. He is usually very punctual. He arrives on the dot at ten o'clock usually."

"Only that? No problem, Sau Jacob! I will call you."

"Thanks, Sau Paul. You are a big help."

At twenty to ten, they began changing into the olive-green army uniforms, which were all complete to the last detail. The stiff belts with shiny buckles, the epaulets, the stars on Jacob's uniform, the medals and the stripes the dark blue berets ... even the spit and polish of the black boots ...it was all there.

"You are looking good, Number 1!" said Number 2 complimenting Jacob.

"Thank you. All of you look very authentic," responded Jacob.

"That's the idea. There's one last detail. We need to have mustaches. All the soldiers from the plains have them."

Number 3 brought around a bunch of fake mustaches and Jacob picked one that fit.

"Too bad there are no mirrors to see myself," said Jacob smiling.

"No, there are," said Number 3 pointing to the side-view mirrors of the Commandant's jeep.

When Jacob walked over to take a look at himself, he laughed out aloud.

"I look funny. It is so strange how such a small detail can make such a big difference," said Jacob.

"That's true. Often it is the small things that matter."

Finally, they slipped on the dark blue berets with the shiny golden federal army badges, each helping the other to adjust the berets to perfection.

By five to ten they were all dressed up and ready. They rolled up their own clothes and placed them in the back of the SNLF jeep.

Number 2 slipped the silencer into the pocket of his trousers and placed the automatic in its holster. Number 3 and Number 4 did likewise. Number 2 handed a pistol to Jacob and said, "Doesn't matter if you don't know how to use this. Just stick it the holster. It's part of the uniform."

Number 4 rolled cigarettes again for his two SNLF colleagues and himself. Just then a taxi headed to town came down the hill.

"We need to act as if we are army soldiers stopping for a break," said Number 2.

They waved at the occupants of the packed taxi but the villagers only glared back.

"Our uniforms seem to be working," commented Jacob.

Waiting was not easy for Jacob. The other three seemed easy and relaxed and he envied them.

The call came at three minutes past ten o'clock.

"Sau Jacob, the DGP just arrived," said Paul.

"Thanks. I will talk to you later," said Jacob ending the call.

"Men, it's time to go," said Jacob decisively.

"We have a ritual before we go into battle," said Number 2.

Jacob followed their actions and held out his right hand. All four stood in a circle with their right hands joined together in a single clasp. With heads bowed they said a silent prayer. After a pause, Number 2 said aloud with great fervor, "Long live Somi Land!" and they all repeated it in unison.

Number 4 got into the driver's seat and Jacob sat in the front seat next to him. Number 2 and Number 3 got into the back seat.

"This jeep is a beauty," said Number 4 as he carefully backed the jeep onto the road. Then after a moment's pause, they were off. They faced no difficulties till they neared the center of the town. The traffic was all backed up and there were no traffic policemen to be seen. As they neared the jam, Jacob curtly told Number 4, "Turn the siren on." Number 4 took some time to locate the switch on the dashboard. When the siren and the flashing red light came on, the traffic quickly dispersed to the sides of the road to make way for the army jeep to pass. They knew the consequences of blocking an army vehicle—and that too of the Commandant's. Jacob's anxiety vanished as they weaved through the clogged traffic and closed in on the Secretariat. Once they reached the vicinity of the Secretariat it was easy. Policemen were deftly controlling the traffic near the government offices and they were given the right of way as they increased speed and headed towards the other end of the massive Secretariat building.

"Turn the siren off and turn left at the next intersection," said A.

"Which office are we going to?" asked Number 2 from the back.

"I can tell you now. It is the Police Headquarters. And our target is none other than the Director General. His name is Jasbir. He is the slimiest of all the bastards from the plains."

"We have heard of him," assured Number 2. "But I hope you have done proper reconnaissance. This place is as tight as a fortress."

"Trust me. Even the best-guarded place has chinks."

"We are now nearing the location. Number 4 will wait in the jeep. After we get off, you will park the jeep facing the exit and in exactly five minutes you will re-start the engine and keep it running."

"Roger," acknowledged Number 4.

"Number 2 and Number 3, you will both come with me. This should take less than ten minutes."

As the jeep neared the front entrance, the gates opened for the Commandant's jeep and they drove in without stopping. Number 2 and Number 3 got out from the rear and Number 4 ran around to Jacob side to hold open the door. When Jacob stepped out of the jeep his heart was thumping wildly.

"Where are the presents for the DGP?" he asked loudly and Number 3 quickly opened the rear flap of the jeep to take out the plastic bag with the *luans*.

At a nod from Jacob, they walked up the steps of the Police Headquarters, with Number 2 and Number 3 flanking Jacob who was a step ahead. Number 3 carried the plastic bag with the *luans* in the palm of his hand held stiffly at right angles to his body.

The reception they received when they reached the entrance was exactly what Jacob had hoped for. Like the army group he had seen being waved through, they were also allowed to enter. Nonetheless, Number 2 walked up to the sergeant at the reception and said loudly in fluent *Dindi*, "Our new Major has come to pay his respects to the Director General. He has brought some very special presents on the suggestion of Colonel Kattar," he said winking. Number 3 held up the packet of *luans* for all to see and they smiled knowingly.

It was a little more than two minutes since they had stepped out of the jeep and they were already climbing the steps to the next floor. Nobody said a word. Soon they turned into the secluded corridor of the right wing.

"Slip the silencer on and place the revolver between the two *luans*," whispered Jacob and Number 2 quickly did as he was told.

When they neared the DGP's room at the end of the corridor, Jacob had a decision to make. Should he go through the office of the Adjutant or should he take a chance and use the direct door outside. If he went in directly there was the possibility of collateral damage if a third party was in the room. He quickly looked at his watch. It was 10:15. He decided to use the direct entrance.

"This is it," whispered Jacob as he gripped the polished brass doorknob and pushed the door in.

The DGP was alone. He was standing near the window flipping through a girlie magazine. Jasbir's mouth opened in surprise at the unexpected entrance.

"Good morning, Director General!" greeted Jacob in English. "We bring you a special gift from the Somi people."

Jacob motioned Number 3 to step forward. Number 3 took a step forward on Jacob's right and held the plastic bag in front of Jacob.

Placing his right hand on top of the bag to keep the contents from falling out, Jacob whisked the bag off with his left hand in one smooth movement, to reveal the two beautiful *luans*.

Mesmerized, Jasbir made as if to step forward to receive the presents. But the look in Jacob's eyes told him that something was not right. He seemed frozen between moving to his desk and pressing the alarm button and stepping forward to receive the beautiful *luans*.

Jacob signaled Number 2 to step up.

Then Jacob looked straight into the eyes of Jasbir and said, "This is a present from the people of the Somi tribe. You have dishonored and shamed our women. You have tortured and killed our young men. You have trampled upon our customs and our values. Now you must pay. Your nemesis has come."

With that, Jacob lifted the red *luan* to reveal the pistol below.

Instinctively, the DGP reached for his revolver.

"Now!" hissed Jacob.

The old man was no match for the speed of the well-trained guerilla. In one deft motion, from Jacob's left, Number 2 took a step forward, picked up the revolver and fired, swinging his arm in the direction of the DGP in one swift arc.

There was a dull thud as the bullet hit the DGP right between the eyes as he lunged toward the shelter of his desk, his slow right hand still on the holster. The white wall behind him suddenly bloomed into a Rorschach splatter of blood and brains as he crumbled backward onto the floor.

"Keep the *luans* on the desk and let's get out of here," said Jacob and moved towards the door through which they had entered. The corridor was empty. Restraining the impulse to run, they walked swiftly towards the stairs in the same formation as they had come.

At the reception, Number 2 waved gaily to the sergeant and his team.

"That was a short visit!" said the sergeant.

"Yes, he can't wait to give the *luans* to his girlfriend," said Number 2 derisively in *Dindi*.

With that, they were outside.

On seeing them, Number 4 brought the idling jeep quickly over to the steps and they all clambered in.

It had taken all of six minutes from the time they came in. Jacob looked at his watch. It was 10:27.

The outward traffic was thin but Jacob did not want to take any chances with oncoming traffic and he leaned over and flicked the siren switch on. With the red roof light flashing and the siren screaming, they sped out of the center of the city. Once they were past the town center Jacob turned the light and the siren off.

They were still some distance from the bridge when they heard the town siren go off.

They knew their act had been discovered and there was not a moment to lose. Leaving the Commandant's jeep on the city side of the bridge they ran down the embankment and through the knee-deep water to the other side tugging at their uniforms. The shirts, belts, and berets were in their hands by the time they reached the haystack and all that remained was to pull off their boots and trousers. The three SNLF men changed into their own clothes but decided there was not time enough to put their shoes on. Barefoot and their shirts still unbuttoned they jumped into their jeep.

"Want to come with us for a few days till things cool down?" asked Number 2.

"No, I cannot. Thank you. You go on ahead. I will be fine. You did an excellent job," said Jacob buttoning his shirt.

"It was all teamwork. You planned it well. Goodbye!"

The three of them waved as the jeep threw up a cloud of dust and accelerated towards the road leading uphill and away from the town.

Jacob hurriedly tied his shoelaces and then slipped on his black leather jacket.

He did not know what to do with the Commandant's jeep.

Rosie's instructions were to bring it back to the spot from where he had taken it. But driving it now was too risky. The police would have radioed the description of the vehicle and he would be nabbed in no time. He decided to leave it where it was and head back to town.

He ran for more than a kilometer before he found a taxi headed in the direction of the town.

The center of the town was crawling with policemen. The city siren had been turned off by then. But people were rushing in different directions. He asked a person hurrying away what had happened. "I don't know. They say the Chief Minister has been killed."

It would be too much of a coincidence, decided Jacob, for both to happen on the same day. He reasoned it must be just the rumors snowballing.

He decided to see what was happening at the Police Headquarters and was headed in that direction when a police van rushed by announcing through a megaphone an immediate and indefinite curfew.

Jacob turned and hurried home.

Everything had happened so quickly. He had had no time to think. He felt exhilarated that his plan had succeeded. The demon had been slain in its own den. The pride of the Somi tribe had been avenged. He had felt no pity at all when the bullet hit the cornered DGP and splattered his brains on the wall. What made him feel guilty was that he had felt no remorse at killing another human being.

When he got home, Ma and Nau Elsie were totally unaware of the situation in the town. He briefly told them that the administration was imposing a curfew in the town. Ma was worried about Edwin. But Jacob told her he would be home soon. Nau Elsie told Jacob that Rosie had called to say she had left a letter for him in her house.

Jacob tried calling Rosie, but all he got was a recorded message saying her phone was 'out of range'.

And indeed, she was.

## Chapter 15

When the Adjutant escorted the three members of the elite society ladies' club into the DGP's room, he was initially nonplussed to see the DGP neither at his desk nor near the window. It was one of the ladies who first noticed his spread-eagled body lying on the ground and she began screaming. And then he saw the blood and gore on the wall.

All hell broke loose then.

The fat lady swooned and collapsed on the carpet. The other two ran back out into the Adjutant's chamber. The Adjutant himself reacted even more dramatically than the women. He opened the door to the corridor and ran towards the left wing shouting, "He has died! He has been killed!"

By the time the senior officers trotted into the DGP's room from the left wing, the lady who had fainted had come out of the swoon and had made it out to the Adjutant's room. The officers initially thought it was a suicide. One of the older officers surreptitiously pocketed the girlie magazine lying on the floor. It was the youngest officer, a direct officer recruit, who made the stunning announcement.

"The DGP has been assassinated. This is not a suicide," the Sub-Divisional Police Officer stated.

"But nobody came to see the DGP today," protested the Adjutant. "The three ladies from the women's club came into the room with me. I was with them."

"That may well be true. But the DGP did not shoot himself. His revolver is still in its holster and I doubt if it has been fired."

This caused even more consternation.

The Deputy DGP decided to take over control of the proceedings. "Sound the alarm. Raise the alert status to 'Code Red' and inform the army. And connect me to the Chief Minister immediately."

The town siren was immediately turned on and the police and security forces scattered around the town knew right away that something ominous had occurred.

*** 

Mohan heard the siren too. He jumped out of bed quaking with fear and began pulling on his uniform hurriedly. His moment of joy had suddenly turned into the worst nightmare.

"Where is my jeep? Where is my jeep? The Commandant will kill me!" he blabbered incoherently.

"I think the jeep will come soon," replied Rosie but she did not care anymore. She knew from the siren that something drastic had occurred, but whether Jacob had been successful or not she did not know.

"I cannot wait for the jeep. I must go look for it," said Mohan running out of the house.

Rosie's ordeal of self-abasement was over.

She phoned Philipson but did not ask him about the siren.

"Sau Philipson, please send the jeep. I am ready to join the defenders of our land," she said.

"Have you not heard? Something terrible has happened. Some VIP has been shot dead," Philipson was uncharacteristically excited. "They are imposing a curfew."

"Really? All the more reason I must get out now. Send the jeep right away."

"How can I do it? I need time," replied Philipson.

"Please, Sau Philipson. You promised me. I need to go now. I have never asked you for a favor. Somehow get me out of the town before they clamp down the curfew," pleaded Rosie.

"All right, for your sake, I will do it. I will send my own jeep with Sau Ben, my personal driver. But I will be without a jeep till he gets back which won't be before the curfew is lifted again."

"Thank you! Thank you! Thank you!" gushed Rosie. "You are very kind. There is one more thing. Please do not tell anyone – not even Sau Jacob – about this."

She then went to the bathroom, quickly bathed in cold water and was ready and waiting when Ben drew up in front of her house.

Ben had more accurate news to share.

"The DGP was assassinated this morning," he said.

"Who killed him do you know?" asked Rosie.

"No one has claimed responsibility but it looks like the job of the SNLF."

"Was the assailant caught?" she asked unable to contain her curiosity.

"No, no one was caught. It was a daring act."

Rosie breathed a huge sigh of relief and a proud smile crossed her face.

They made it out of town in the nick of time just as the curfew was being enforced.

Once they were past the last checkpoint, she relaxed. She told herself her sacrifice had not been in vain. She was not sure, though, if she could ever bring herself to marry Jacob. What had happened was irrevocable. Something had forever been lost. She considered herself now married to her land.

A short while later she pulled out the SIM card of her cell phone and threw it out of the window.

\*\*\*

It was again the Sub-Divisional Police Officer who noticed the two *luans* on the table. There was no blood on them. He looked around for a message of some sort but did not find any.

"Who brought these *luans* to the DGP?" he asked the Adjutant.

"I don't know. They were not here yesterday. The ladies' club members did not bring them. That much I know for a fact," he said.

The young Sub-Divisional Police Officer then deduced that the *luans* were themselves the message.

"Call the reception and ask if there had been any visitors to meet the DGP today," directed the Deputy DGP.

"Nobody came today except the ladies' club committee," crackled the voice of the sergeant over the intercom.

"Are you sure there was nobody else?" persisted the Deputy DGP.

"No, sir. No one. No civilians." Then he remembered the new army major and his two assistants. "No one except the group from the army."

"What group?" asked the Deputy DGP.

"There was the new army major with two junior commissioned officers."

"What was the major's name?" asked the Deputy DGP.

"I did not write it down. Since they were from the army I let them through," the sergeant whined.

"You idiot! How can you be sure they were from the army? Did you check with the cantonment? Did you recognize either of the junior commissioned officers?"

"No, sir." The sergeant's voice was almost inaudible. He realized that he had committed a serious blunder.

"Were they carrying any gifts for the DGP?" interposed the Sub-Divisional Police Officer unable to contain his curiosity.

"Yes, sir. They brought two *luans* as gifts for the DGP."

The Deputy DGP turned intercom off.

"We have been royally duped," he said wearily. "Heads will roll for this serious breach of security."

"Request permission to go down to the reception and examine the staff," said the Sub-Divisional Police Officer.

"Permission granted." He then turned to the Director of Security, "Place the entire team on security duty this morning under suspension and grill them till we find the culprits. Have the body removed to the government hospital. I will talk to the Chief Minister from my chamber," he said walking out.

It was the Sub-Divisional Police Officer who turned up the evidence of the Commandant's jeep. He was initially inclined to discount it as a figment of the guard's imagination. It was inconceivable that the army would execute the chief of police. The constable at the gate swore that it was the Commandant's own jeep and not a fake. "But," he added, "the driver was different."

An alert was immediately sounded for the Commandant's jeep.

Mohan, disheveled and disoriented, was within two kilometers of the safety of the cantonment when he was nabbed by the Federal Reserve Police. On leaving Rosie's house he had hired a taxi and, out of desperation, driven all around the small town looking for the Commandant's jeep. His joy knew no bounds when he spotted it unscathed and undamaged near the bridge. Unfortunately, his luck ran out when the Federal Reserve Police intercepted him within striking distance of the camp. His answers were incoherent and inconsistent. Since they had no powers to arrest a soldier of the army, the cantonment was immediately informed. The military police quickly arrived on the scene and whisked him away for interrogation.

\*\*\*

The call that Jacob had been waiting for came shortly after two o'clock in the afternoon.

"Bravo! Congratulations on a job well done!"

"Thank you, General Thanga. I am happy that the operation went as planned. Your boys did an excellent job," replied Jacob.

"You did an amazing job! This is unbelievable! I want you to know that you have the respect and admiration of the entire Somi tribe. Our Chief Commander is really happy. He said it was the happiest day of his life. His said this act of bravery will live forever in the annals of the Somi tribe."

"Thank you, General. I don't deserve all this praise. I was only doing my duty," said Jacob modestly.

"If half of our young men would do a hundredth of what you have done for our cause, we would be a free nation," said General Thanga.

"I agree, we all need to work harder."

"Anyway, I want to let you know that the SNLF will claim responsibility for this. You will be completely protected. Your name will not be mentioned at all. Does anybody there know of your involvement in this?"

"No, no one."

"Are you sure? What about Sau Philipson?" persisted the General.

"No, he doesn't know. I kept my word. I didn't tell a soul," confirmed Jacob again.

"Well, if at any time you think your role will be discovered, just let us know and we will pick you up. It will be jungle life for you from then on till it is safe for you to go back," said General Thanga.

"OK. I am ready for that. But if I stayed here I could do more."

"I know. But we must also think of your personal safety and that of our cause. We don't want our work destroyed."

"No, that's true. If there is a risk, I will get out of here. I just remembered. There is one other person who knows about what happened today."

"Who's this?" asked General suddenly wary.

"No, don't worry. It is my closest friend. She will never leak the story to anyone. She played a part in today's operation but she doesn't know the whole story. At least not yet."

"Is she safe?" asked the General.

"I think so. I have been trying to get through to her but I guess she is out of cell phone range."

"What is her name?"

"Her name is Rosie. She is my girlfriend."

There was a pause at the other end.

"Sau Jacob, I will call you back. Something just came up," said General Thanga switching off.

*** 

A short while later, a phone call was received at the Somi Times newspaper. The caller, claiming to be from SNLF, made a brief statement that he insisted be written down and published verbatim. The copy read: "The Somi National Liberation Front proudly claims responsibility for the gunning down of the Director General of Police in his office at 10:24 this morning. The DGP was executed for the crimes he committed against the Somi people. May his killing be a warning to all other evildoers who are working to suppress the just cause of our freedom and independence. This is a final warning to the occupiers and the agents of the puppet government. You cannot hide. If you do wrong, we will hunt you out and kill you. Long live our Mother Land!"

The caller then added, "When you inform the police be sure to mention the *luans*."

From the communication desk at the city's main police station, the message was relayed to the Sub-Divisional Officer of Police. He knew immediately that the message was genuine; the time of the killing (not publicly announced at that time) matched the chain of events and the timeline perfectly. The clincher, of course, was the reference to the *luans*.

A Somi himself, he felt a twinge of admiration for the precision and audacity of the maneuver.

"If we had intelligent and courageous men like them in the police force, what could we not achieve?" he asked himself rhetorically.

\*\*\*

Chief Minister Chapang was visibly rattled. SNLF had struck at the heart of the administration. If the well-guarded DGP could be killed, he was not safe either.

He immediately clamped down an indefinite curfew and then called the federal capital and requested army and Federal Reserve Police reinforcements.

He then called his trusted lieutenant to discuss the possibility of making a secret payoff to the SNLF to buy protection.

\*\*\*

The army acted swiftly.

A wire went out recalling Colonel Kattar from his furlough.

A flag march was called out in the main streets of the town and additional check posts were set up.

The message was clear. The police were inefficient and could not be trusted. The army had to be in charge.

As the curfew was being enforced, stragglers were roughed up and manhandled.

The soldiers cooped up too long in their barracks waited eagerly for nightfall to satisfy their libido.

\*\*\*

The police force was shamefaced and demoralized. The killing of their chief was the worst form of insult imaginable. More than anything else, it reinforced the army's categorization of the police force as an incompetent, blundering force that could not be relied upon. The incident also tested the loyalty of Somi policemen. On the one hand, they had to bear the ignominy of the killing of their chief but, on the other, many of them were elated that the wicked and depraved leader had been eliminated in such daring fashion.

But the damage was done. In one fell swoop, they had been demoted to being the lackeys of the army and the Federal Reserve Police. As darkness fell, it was the police who, like guide dogs, led the army to the houses of suspected militants and sympathizers. The provincial police force had been reduced to being mere guides and interpreters. Worse, the police, more than half of whom were Somis, had to mutely watch the army's highhanded actions against their own people.

*\*\*\**

The response of the army was brutal. Able-bodied young men were pounded with rifle butts and kicked with heavy army boots when they fell writhing in pain to the ground. The presence of family, women, and children did not soften their viciousness. The army entered homes with scant respect for civility or decency. Their modus operandi was to herd the family into one room while they ransacked the rest of the house. The soldiers pocketed money and anything of value they could stuff in their pockets. They handled the prized possessions of the owners with the utter lack of respect typical of uncultured boors. Worse, they brazenly fondled girls and women in full view of their parents, husbands, siblings and children. It was as if there was no law or morals to temper their barbarity. The provincial policemen were reduced to being impotent bystanders seething with inward rage as they watched their brethren being savaged.

*\*\*\**

The army never came to Jacob's house. He knew he was regarded as harmless and was not on the police list. He also knew that his disguise earlier in the day, handlebar mustache and all, had not been seen through. But he was worried for Rosie's safety. There was no way he could go out to her house to look for her. The police announcement of curfew earlier had also mentioned the cancellation of all curfew passes. There was no option. He would have to wait out the night. He was debating whether to call Philipson or not when his cell phone rang. It was Philipson.

"Did you hear what happened? The SNLF killed the DGP in his own office. What a daring attack!" said Philipson excitedly.

"Yes, I heard. The pig deserved to die," said Jacob without emotion.

"This has scared the government. I heard they have requested the federal government for three more battalions of army and two battalions of the Federal Reserve Police force."

"It is time the government woke up and stopped the atrocities of the army and the police. We are being pushed to the wall," said Jacob.

"I think worse is to come. The government has handed over control of the town to the army. The federal government will come down on us with a heavy hand. I won't be surprised if they call in the air force to bomb us like they did to our neighbors the Remas."

"The more they punish us, the greater will be the alienation," said Jacob.

"I know, but think of the suffering ..."

"What do they call it in military terms? Collateral damage? I hope they don't use too much force. They will pay for it later,' said Jacob.

"I think we must negotiate so we can have peace again," suggested Philipson.

"Negotiate? Never! The blood of our slaughtered brethren will cry out from the ground."

"Anyway, you must be relieved that SNLF did the job and not you," said Philipson.

"The SNLF are the professionals. I am glad they did this daring job," replied Jacob evasively, secretly glad that Philipson did not know of his involvement.

"Anyway, when the curfew is lifted I have more money to give you. I received a lot of donations during the previous week."

"OK. I will come as soon as the curfew is relaxed. I am sure SNLF will need more funds after this."

"Is Rosie's mother staying with you?" asked Philipson.

"Nau Elsie? Yes, why?" asked Jacob surprised.

"No reason," said Philipson.

*** 

The curfew stayed in place for the whole of the following day. This was standard army procedure, Jacob knew, to demoralize the population and undermine their support for the underground. The federal government hoped to break the will of the people and persuade them to oppose the SNLF by starving the children and poor families. It was, as usual, the daily-wage earners who suffered the most. They needed a full day's work to earn their living and would not have enough money to buy food when the curfew was relaxed for a few hours.

The twice-daily news in the Somi language on the national radio had only a brief mention of the killing of the Director General of Police. The news was mainly about the curfew and how strictly it was being enforced. Shoot-at-sight orders had been issued for the night hours.

Jacob spent the time lying motionless on his bed with his eyes closed. He looked back over the direction his life had taken and he was not happy. The sense of elation at successfully masterminding the most intrepid attack on the establishment was beginning to fade. The joy of excelling at something totally out of his ken was being replaced by a sense of futility and a sense of despair with the realization that the forces he was fighting against were too powerful and entrenched. He looked at Ché's book Guerilla Warfare and wondered if Ché had felt the same way after his successes.

On the third day, the curfew was relaxed for two hours from nine in the morning. As people made a beeline for the shops to buy rice and provisions, the army stayed in control patrolling the streets. It was mostly old men and women accompanied by children who went shopping. Able-bodied young men stayed home for fear of being picked up for interrogation.

Ma and Edwin had gone to the shop when Jacob's cell phone rang. It was General Thanga. He went to his room and shut the door. He was not sure whether Rosie's mother would overhear but that was a risk he had to take.

"Sau Jacob, I have some very bad news for you. I have reliable information that the army arrested more than one hundred of our young men in the town. I don't have the exact number. These are figures we got from different localities. We also received word that soldiers gang-raped three of our women last night. We will know the truth only when the curfew is relaxed further."

"I feel very guilty for bringing this tragedy on my own tribe," said Jacob contritely.

"You must not feel that way. You did the bravest act in the history of this conflict. There's something else I must tell you," said General Thanga gravely.

"What can be worse news than this?' asked Jacob despondently.

"Rosie enlisted. She is with us," said the General gently.

"What?" Jacob thought his head would explode.

"She joined the day the DGP was liquidated."

"Is she there? Can I talk to her?" asked Jacob desperately.

"No, she is isn't here with me right now. And she doesn't want to talk to anyone. You must give her time."

Jacob did not hear any more of what the General said. He sat numbly with the cell phone in his hand.

He looked at his watch. There were still fifty minutes left before the curfew was enforced again.

He left the house without telling Nau Elsie. He picked up Rosie's house keys from the kitchen and ran like a madman all the way to Rosie's house.

He found the letter on her mother's bed.

Jacob ripped open the envelope and read. When he came to the part about the price she paid for getting the Commandant's jeep, tears rolled down his face and it was all he could do to keep from bawling out. She had ended her letter with, "Goodbye Strelnikov, my darling! If we should never meet again, know that I always loved you and only you."

He crumpled the letter into a ball and threw it against the wall and punched the wooden posts of the door. Then, he sank to the floor and held his throbbing head in his bleeding hands.

After a while, he got up, washed his face, picked up the balled-up letter and carefully smoothened it out. He folded it carefully and slipped it into the inside pocket of his leather jacket. He then walked home with a new resoluteness.

The authorities had relented and extended the relaxation of the curfew by another hour.

He waited till Ma and Edwin ad returned home.

Then, after they had had tea with bowls of beaten rice, Jacob broke the news.

Rosie's mother almost fainted. Ma rushed to her side and held her saying repeatedly, "Don't worry. Rosie will be all right. She will come back."

Jacob slowly stood up and pushed the low bamboo stool back. He could not bear to keep it secret anymore.

"Ma, Rosie is not alone. I am on the other side too."

He saw the bowl slip from Edwin's hands and crash to the floor.

Ma's bewildered face dissolved in tears as she remembered the premonition she had had in the garden about Jacob's death.

"Don't go, son, don't go," she whimpered.

"Ma, I am not going now but we all need to fight for our freedom."

"I knew you were up to something. How did you forget everything your father and I taught you?"

Then she added resignedly, "What is the point in suffering like this? Isn't food and shelter enough? What more freedom do you want?"

"When will my daughter come back?" wailed Nau Elsie.

Jacob had no answer to any of these questions. Edwin sat with his face buried in his hands sobbing silently.

## Chapter 16

Colonel Kattar was deeply unhappy at being recalled from his leave. He was even more outraged that his jeep had been used for the treacherous act against the government. He ordered the rigorous interrogation of the driver, Mohan, suspecting him to have received financial payoffs in return for his collaboration. A search of his personal effects had revealed nothing. Mohan resolutely stuck to his story: after dropping Rosie off at her house, he had taken a woman he had met in the market to the secluded area near the bridge and the jeep had been by the roadside all the time. He said he did not remember whether he had left the key in the ignition or not. They pressed him for the name of the woman but his defense was that she was a market harlot and it was the first and the last time he had seen her. Mohan knew that if he told the truth about his tryst with Rosie his life would be at risk. The colonel, he knew, was capable of staging a mock encounter and having him bumped off in a jealous rage for stealing Rosie's affections.

The Sub-Divisional Officer who sat in on the interrogation knew that Mohan was not telling the whole truth. But no amount of coercion or third degree could force Mohan to change his story. The canine team was sent down to the spot where Mohan said he had parked the jeep but the trail had run cold by then. The young police officer was not one to give up so easily. When he crossed the bridge and reached the haystack, he discovered the tire marks of another vehicle and indications that it might have been the staging place. But no further clues could be found.

Colonel Kattar was eager to meet Rosie again to find out about SNLF plans and to tell her about his trip. But all he got was the out-of-range message that Jacob had got earlier. He also realized that he did not know where Rosie lived. It was Mohan the driver who always took her back home and he was now in custody.

Colonel Kattar decided that offense was the best form of defense. At the next security meeting, he outlined his plan to the Chief Minister. "Sir, the attackers have already left the city. Extending the curfew will not help us to capture them. While the army is deployed in the city the underground elements outside the city have an easy time re-grouping themselves for another attack. I recommend that the patrolling of the city be handed over to the Federal Reserve Police. Then I can move the new battalions and almost the entire camp into the jungle to fight the militants. We can wipe them out completely. Annihilate them totally. We need to show them who's in power by killing twenty of their men for each one of our army men or policemen killed."

"They killed the Director General—not an ordinary constable," corrected Chief Minister Chapang.

"For the DGP we should kill at least fifty rebels," said Colonel Kattar emphatically.

"How confident are you about this plan?" asked the Chief Minister skeptically.

"Completely! I will personally lead the forces for this operation. Before this posting, I was the principal of the Counter Insurgency and Jungle Warfare School. I know how to survive in the jungle," Colonel Kattar boasted.

Chief Minister Chapang wanted nothing more than the elimination of the threat to his life from the insurgents. Showing the federal government that he dealt firmly with the rebellion and brought peace would mean more federal funds for the province and hence more opportunities for increasing his own personal wealth.

Chief Minister Chapang readily approved the plan and Colonel Kattar moved his camp temporarily to the edge of the jungle over the next few days.

***

As life in the town limped back to normalcy, Jacob resumed where he had left off. He managed the finances for the Movement and kept accounts as he had before. But somehow his heart was no longer in it. "If only Rosie were back," he said to himself many times. The work had become just a routine job now. Strelnikov had lost his passion. Many times, he considered signing up for the underground. It was only the thought of his mother and brother that held him back. There was also Rosie's mother to be taken care of now. Nau Elsie had insisted on returning to her house to live alone but Ma and Jacob would have none of it. When he gave funds to the emissaries from the underground he tried to send letters to Rosie through them. They took his letters but he never got a reply.

He even called General Thanga once to seek his help but the response he got was noncommittal.

"Sau Jacob, you have to give her some time. She must get it out of her system. Maybe she considers this jungle life some sort of penance, I don't know. But right now, she does not want any contacts with anyone outside her immediate team."

"Is she OK? Is she healthy?" asked Jacob.

"Yes, she is. She is perfectly fine and has adapted well to the rigors of training. She had a problem with mosquitoes but she is taking anti-malarial tablets now."

"How did she reach your camp that day? Did she come with the team I worked with?" asked Jacob.

"No, she came about two hours after them. It was Sau Philipson who arranged her trip. He does it for all our recruits."

Jacob felt immensely sad that Philipson knew all along about Rosie's disappearance but had not shared it with him. But when he thought more about it, he realized that he had likewise kept many secrets from Philipson and that it was all part of the game they were playing. Nonetheless, he felt betrayed.

*** 

The investigations of the Sub-Divisional Officer of Police had reached a dead-end. Unless fresh evidence or information was forthcoming there was very little he could do. But of one thing he was certain. The mastermind behind the DGP's murder could not have been a regular underground militant. Subtlety and strategy were not their forte. Their modus operandi was ambushes and skirmishes in jungle terrain that they knew like the back of their hand. This attack was different. It was carried deep into unfamiliar territory and planned with such precision and lateral thinking that the Sub-Divisional Officer of Police thought an army officer had to be behind the planning. The use of the army vehicle and the disguise of army uniforms all seemed to lend credence to this theory. But the basic assumption itself was so preposterous that he began to look for other evidence that might support it. He reasoned the cause to be either love or money and began secretly probing into the lifestyle and connections of army officers who were possible gamblers or womanizers.

*** 

Some days later Jacob received a call from Paul, his trusted collection agent.

"Sau Jacob, I think I have found out who is collecting money in our name," said Paul.

"Who is doing this?" asked Jacob.

"We both happened to be in the Department of Youth Affairs at the same time. When I realized that we were both there for the same purpose of collecting donations for our cause, I invited him out to tea. After much talking, we agreed to share information."

"You did? Whose name did you give?" asked Jacob slightly alarmed.

"Rest easy, sir! I did not mention your name. I told him I was the direct collection agent for our Chief Commander."

"And who did he say he was collecting for?" asked Jacob.

"You will be surprised, Sau Jacob."

"Tell me who it is," said Jacob impatiently.

"It is Sau Philipson, Sau Jacob," said Paul.

"What!" exclaimed Jacob, unable to hide his astonishment.

"It is true. I made him swear he was telling me the truth. I suggest that you and Sau Philipson decide on specific collection areas so that there will be no overlap. It makes us look bad in the eyes of the public," suggested Paul.

"That's right," agreed Jacob deciding quickly that it is best if he did not share his fears with Paul. "Sorry for the confusion. We will sort this out soon."

Jacob decided to go and take a look at the accounts to see how much Philipson had been withholding as his expenses. It was not what he had anticipated. Philipson had ceased holding back money for his expenses. The earlier amount of six hundred thousand katas or twelve thousand dollars had remained practically stagnant. But Jacob knew that Philipson not deducting his expenses did not prove anything. He knew he had no way of knowing how much Philipson had received in the first place. Philipson's recent purchase of an imported SUV had raised questions about his source of funds.

Jacob decided it was time he had a heart to heart talk with Philipson regarding the allegation he had just heard.

***

Colonel Kattar thirsted for revenge. It was not anything personal. But the enemy's attack had been a slap in the face of the government and he was not one to take an insult lying down. He decided that with the additional forces at his disposal he could afford the luxury of a pincer attack on the enemy. The insurgents would be caught in the valley in the middle while the army would be on the hills on either side. The militants would be sitting ducks. He divided his forces into two teams and sent them on their way.

Towards dusk, he heard the sound of distant gunfire. The news that came over the radio was not good. They had been caught in an ambush in a bamboo grove and eight soldiers had been killed and many injured. It was almost midnight when the injured and the dead were brought to base camp. The colonel vowed revenge and kept swilling whiskey. At dawn, fresh reinforcements were sent. The other team on the east side had faced no opposition.

The weeks of training in jungle warfare had only partially prepared the soldiers for what they faced. By the third day their water and food rations had run out and they were forced to resort to the survival methods they had been taught. The eating of rodents and diverse birds and the drinking of mountain springs did nothing to boost the morale of the troops as they battled heat and humidity during the day and mosquitoes at night.

It was on the afternoon of the third day that an alert scout on the eastern wing spotted a thin plume of smoke near the stream that flowed down the middle of the valley. A radio message was sent to the base camp for relaying to the troops on the western front who were on the other side of the mountain and out of direct radio contact. The western team quickly climbed to the top of the mountain and established direct radio contact with the team on the eastern ridge. The two arms of the pincer slowly closed in on the valley. In the mellow afternoon light, powerful binoculars spotted the rebel camp on the western bank of the stream. There must have been about thirty of them totally oblivious to the impending danger. Some of the men had laid out their clothes on the ground to dry. A few (possibly women) were cooking food over a low fire. It was the smoke of this fire that had given them away. The western team climbed lower down the mountain and waited for their counterparts also to descend to stream-level on the eastern side to cut off any escape route.

Then, without warning the western team opened fire on the unsuspecting underground militia. It was murder in cold blood. The hail of bullets mowed down those sitting in the open. Those who tried to escape by crossing the stream were shot down by the team on the opposite bank. They were completely cornered. Only the ones on the periphery had any chance. Two of them jumped into the river and swam downstream underwater till they were far enough from the conflict area. The others on the edge ran back into the forest. Within minutes it was all over. On the banks of the river lay the bodies of twenty-three men and three women. A radio message was sent to base camp. Colonel Kattar was jubilant at his success. He ordered the men to guard the site and leave things exactly as they were till he arrived. He then radioed the good news to Chief Minister Chapang and requested the use of the government helicopter and the services the media team from the Department of Public Relations.

The jungle was eerily quiet with the smell of death. Blood stained the white sand and the brown earth but the water ran clear. A soldier went to the shirtless body of a young man and kicked the body to make sure it was dead before searching for gold or other valuables. The major immediately stopped him. He allowed the hungry men to take the cooked fish but did not allow them to touch any of the bodies.

The helicopter took only forty minutes to arrive overhead before slowly descending to the riverbank in the early evening light. The man with the video camera walked around the perimeter of the carnage recording the scene from every angle. He continued to shoot as the colonel took his sunglasses off and went from body to body posing for the camera. A soldier turned over bodies that lay face down shot from the back. Not one of the bodies held a gun or was within reach of one. The colonel reached the three female bodies lying close to the dead embers of the fire. The women had apparently been barbecuing fish for the group. All three lay face down with their heads towards the river. They had all been shot from behind. The one in the middle had been shot in the head and back. When the soldier turned her over, the face was unrecognizable, the bullets having blown off chunks of flesh when they exited.

Something glittered in the fading sunlight and the colonel bent down to take a closer look. Even in the deepening gloom of twilight he easily recognized the gold chain and the tiny cross.

A mere glance at the rest of the body was enough to confirm his worst fears.

It was Rosie.

He nearly retched and was grateful for the gloom that hid his facial reaction. He slipped his dark glasses on again in spite of the deepening dusk.

## Chapter 17

A pall of gloom descended on the SNLF camp when the two men who escaped by swimming underwater brought the sad news to General Thanga and the Chief Commander. It was presumed that the other twenty-nine had been killed. The presence of the two army units made it too risky to send a team to recover the bodies and bury the dead honorably. The Chief Commander chastised General Thanga for the lack of intelligence on the army surge. General Thanga, for his part, responded swiftly by temporarily suspending all operations and ordering all personnel to move to safe havens.

The word of the 'encounter' reached the city. The national news that night mentioned a 'fierce battle' and the 'victory' of the army. Colonel Kattar received congratulatory messages from Chief Minister Chapang and the federal government.

Colonel Kattar's glory, however, was short-lived, lasting only a few weeks. The video recording that had captured his moment of glory proved to be his undoing. An international human rights organization that examined the video exposed the cold-blooded killings. The evidence was incontrovertible. The two majors who led the assault teams were court-martialed. Colonel Kattar himself was acquitted of wrongdoing but was asked to proceed on retirement.

***

The next day three more of the men turned up alive. They were on the periphery and had escaped death by quickly climbing up to the upper reaches of the tall trees. The army had combed the forest but their search had proved fruitless. The three survivors confirmed the deaths of their comrades and the fact that the army had conducted a mass cremation of the bodies the next morning before moving on.

SNLF conveyed the news of the deaths to the relatives of the deceased. General Thanga personally called Jacob to offer his condolences. Jacob was inconsolable. He buried his face in his pillow and wept uncontrollably. He did not know how to break the news to Nau Elsie and to Ma. He blamed himself for Rosie's humiliation and death. The sweet savor of victory had changed to the bitter, ashen taste of personal defeat.

Suddenly Jacob had had enough of idealism and patriotism. He decided to give it all up. He did not care if he had freedom or not. He did not care anymore whether his tribe survived or whether it was assimilated into the mainstream of the nation. All these were beyond his control. He should never have worried about all this in the first place. His mind was made up. He would go and personally tell Philipson. He would sever all connections with the SNLF too.

It was early evening when he slipped out of the house. He took a taxi to Philipson's house but he wasn't home. Ben the driver told him Philipson was at a meeting at the Evening Club. Jacob took a taxi to the city center and walked to the EC. He had never liked the atmosphere of clubs. Cigarette smoke hung thick in the air and the place reeked of alcohol. The Club was packed with government officers, businessmen, and fashionably dressed women. To Jacob, this was all a colossal waste of time and money, to say nothing of other immoral temptations that this atmosphere spawned. He looked around for Philipson but could not find him. When he inquired from the manager he was told that Philipson was at a meeting on the second floor and couldn't be disturbed. Jacob did not have time. This could not wait. He had to do it now.

Unnoticed, he climbed the service stairs to the second floor and walked down the corridor. All the rooms were quiet. When he neared the very end, he heard animated voices and laughter from behind the last door. He knocked lightly and heard a voice say, "It's open! Come on in."

Jacob turned the knob and stepped in.

What met his eyes stunned him. Sitting around a large table were Chief Minister Chapang, Colonel Kattar, the Deputy Director General of Police, the Chief Secretary to the provincial government, four of the richest Warbari businessmen and Philipson. Piled high, in the middle of the table, were stacks of currency in thousand and five-hundred kata notes. Young Somi girls sat on sofas around the room in varying stages of tipsiness. Everyone turned to him in surprise.

It was Colonel Kattar who broke the impasse. "You are not the waiter, are you?"

"No," he replied. "I'm not. I came to see Sau Philipson but I think I have seen enough."

Philipson sighed as he put both hands palm down on the edge of the table and pushed his chair back.

"This is not what you think it is. Let me explain ..." said Philipson rising up.

"Not what I think?" Jacob was livid. "Am I blind? You are a traitor! That's what you are. A traitor to the Somi tribe and to our cause," Jacob shouted brandishing his right fist in the air. "You won't hesitate to sell your own mother, you scum! That's what you have done. You have sold our motherland to these vultures sitting with you. You are feeding on our flesh and blood, you bastard! Dividing up the spoils with the vultures of politicians, the army, the police, the bureaucracy and the bloodsucking Warbari dogs, are you? You have blood on your hands, Sau Philipson. The blood of innocents you cheated while you amassed all this wealth. I have nothing but scorn for you. I never imagined you would be in cahoots with these pigs."

Philipson had in the meantime walked up to Jacob and reached out to remonstrate.

"Don't touch me! Don't touch me with those bloodstained hands. I swear I will kill you if you touch me," shouted Jacob stepping back. "Do you know how many of our young people you have led to the slaughter like lambs? Do you know? Do you even care? It is all finished for me today," panted Jacob trying to keep himself from breaking down. He did not succeed. Tears coursing down his face he said, "You and that army bastard ... the two of you ... you killed my Rosie." At the mention of Rosie's name Colonel Kattar started. "I have nothing more to fight for now. Nothing to lose either. Your treachery can never be forgiven. I will tell all. I will publish the truth. It will be in the newspapers. You wait and see. Look around you. You are selling our young girls to these vultures. You won't get away with this as long as I am alive. I will make you pay for your sins."

With that, he turned and left the room.

The silence in the room was palpable. The girls had moved to the back of the room and were cowering together. Philipson nodded his head in the direction of the door and the girls trooped out picking up their handbags lying around on the sofas.

"Who is that fellow?" asked Chief Minister Chapang irritably. "How did he get in here?"

"He is one of my assistants. An idealist, as you just saw. Very hot-headed," explained Philipson clearly embarrassed and annoyed.

"How did he get in here? Where is the security?" asked the Chief Minister.

"Sir, to avoid attention I asked the security team to wait behind the club. If they were inside the club all would know that we were here," said the Deputy Director General of Police apologetically.

"Utter nonsense!" said the Chief Minister dismissively. "What if he had a gun just now?"

"No, sir. He is not dangerous. He is a dreamer. He wanted to kill the DGP. Can you believe that?" snorted Philipson derisively.

"Was he involved in the killing?" asked Colonel Kattar perking up.

"The DGP was killed by the hit squad of SNLF – not this weakling," said Philipson contemptuously.

"How much does he know?" asked Chief Minister Chapang.

"He knows a lot but he is harmless," said Philipson.

"You can never be sure. Kill him!" said the Chief Minister.

"That may be too extreme, sir. He has a mother and a brother," said Philipson.

"We cannot afford to take any chances. He has seen us. He knows too much. If he cannot be bought, kill him," said Chief Minister Chapang.

*** 

Everything was a red blur as Jacob rushed home. Like a madman, he grabbed the shovel and ran to the banana grove. He dug out the tin box with the pistol and leveled the earth again with his bare hands. He was so fixated on what he was doing that he did not see Ma watching him from outside the house. As he neared the house carrying the tin box and the shovel, she asked him, "What is in the box, son?"

"Nothing, Ma," mumbled Jacob as he dropped the shovel and went into his room.

He opened the box on the bed and unwrapped the plastic wrapping. The shiny dark gray pistol felt like a toy as he loaded it. Then he looked up to see his mother standing at the door.

"Son, don't do it," she said firmly. "He who lives by the sword will die by the sword."

"Ma, you don't know what is happening to our land. The wicked flourish while the righteous perish." He seemed to consider for a moment whether or not to tell. Then taking a deep breath he whispered, "They killed Rosie."

"No!" cried Ma stifling her mouth with the cloth apron. "How can we tell Nau Elsie?"

"I don't know, Ma. But I want revenge. It is too complicated, Ma."

"Don't do it, son. Leave revenge to God. If I lose you, I have nothing left."

"No, Ma. Forgive me but I cannot live with this. At least for Rosie's sake, I must kill Sau Philipson."

"Kill Sau Philipson? Are you out of your mind? He is rich and powerful and he has guards."

"I cannot let him live, Ma," Jacob was weeping now unashamedly.

Ma walked up to him and held him close till he calmed down.

"I will go to the garden, Ma. I want to talk to my friend."

Under the shade of the pomegranate and magnolia trees, he felt calm. With deliberateness, he called General Thanga and told him all. The General was not as stunned by the revelation as Jacob had expected him to be.

"I was informed of his double-dealings some time ago. He is under our watch. We are trying to find out what his role was in the intelligence failure that led to the deaths of twenty-six of our brave soldiers. If he betrayed us he will have to die. There are no other options."

"For the sake of Rosie, I am going to kill him today," said Jacob matter-of-factly.

"No, don't do it. Leave that to us. We will take care of him," said General Thanga.

"No, I need justice now, General. Justice is crying in the streets. Justice cannot wait," insisted Jacob.

"That is not a wise thing to do. You are risking your life. He has guards. You are not familiar with arms and ammunition," cautioned the General.

"I don't care. I am past caring. I am going to kill him if it is the last thing I do," said Jacob and ended the call.

\*\*\*

Ma had in the meantime slipped out of the house by the front door. She hurried to Philipson's house. Philipson was not at home. She insisted that she be allowed to speak to Philipson on the cell phone.

"Sau, I am Jacob's mother. Jacob is very upset about the death of Rosie. He is angry with you. He has a gun. Please protect yourself. But please don't harm Jacob. He is innocent. He is all I have got."

"Thank you for warning me, Nau. Your son is a close friend of mine. I will deal with this," said Philipson.

Ma walked home lost in thought. How would she tell Rosie's mother about Rosie's death? How could she calm her son down so he would not do anything foolish?

\*\*\*

Philipson made his decision. Jacob would have to be eliminated. But he did not want to use his own guards for the kill. He was thinking of hiring an assassin when he hit upon a brilliant idea. He went to the terrace of the Evening Club and called Kamat.

"Sau Kamat, I have a job for you. Can you do it?"

"But of course! I have been bored doing nothing for weeks. What kind of a job?" asked Kamat.

"I want you to eliminate a troublemaker."

"No problem. When?"

"Today. Now. Right now."

"OK. Who is the target?" asked Kamat eager for action.

There was a brief pause at the other end.

"It is Sau Jacob," said Philipson without emotion.

"What?" Kamat exclaimed in astonishment.

"He has become too big for his boots. He has to go. Don't tell anyone about this. It will be our secret," said Philipson conspiratorially.

"OK."

"Lie in wait in the lane near his house that leads to the main road. Kill him near his own house. Don't kill him anywhere close to my house. I don't want anyone blaming me for his death. Don't get caught. That is important. How much do you want?" asked Philipson.

"I don't know. How much can you give Sau Philipson?"

"How about twenty-five thousand?"

"That is more than what I expected," snickered Kamat.

\*\*\*

General Thanga paced the floor. He was troubled by what he had learned. He wanted to save Jacob from harm. Jacob was an invaluable asset of the Movement. There was none else like him. The General's dilemma was whether to capture Philipson alive and grill him or to liquidate him summarily. He decided on the latter course as that would take the wind out of Jacob's sails. Jacob would not have any target left for his anger if Philipson was removed. Philipson was corrupt to the core. He would have to go. Jacob was brilliant and patriotic. He had to be saved at all costs.

Using the radio patch General Thanga called Major Kapwanga, known to Jacob as Number 2.

"Where are you now, Major Kapwanga?"

"I am at my mother's house in the city, General Thanga. You told us to lie low and I decided to spend this time with my mother. The house needs many repairs and I have not been with my mother for a long time."

"That is good. But I have an urgent job for you. It has come up rather suddenly. I want you to snuff out someone."

"I am alone. Do I need a backup, General?"

"There is no time for that. The target has a well-guarded house. The Achilles heel is the gate. You must catch him at the gate. The car has to stop for the gate to be opened."

\*\*\*

The wait had cooled Jacob's head. He decided not to act in haste but bide his time to take revenge on Philipson.

Ma called them to have tea. Ma and Jacob avoided the eyes of Rosie's mother. They did not know how to break the news.

"I am going out, Ma," said Jacob pushing the bamboo stool into the corner.

"You better stay home today, son," said Ma unable to hide her anxiety.

"Don't worry, Ma. My pockets are empty," said Jacob patting the pockets of his jacket and jeans. "That thing is under my mattress. I will put it away tonight after I get back. And I will return it next week to the people who gave it to me."

"What is that in your hand, son?" asked Ma.

"This is just a book," said Jacob holding up Ché Guevara's Guerilla Warfare. "I am going to throw this into the river. I don't need this book anymore."

\*\*\*

He was only a hundred feet from his house when Kamat stepped out of the shadows of the trees. Jacob was startled.

"Sau Kamat! What are you doing here?" Jacob asked smiling.

"Waiting for you," answered Kamat as he whipped out his pistol. Jacob instinctively shouldered arms to protect himself. But the bullet was faster. It thudded into his chest and threw him backward onto the unpaved road, his hands flung to either side.

\*\*\*

Ma heard the shot as she was collecting the cups and saucers for washing. She dropped everything and ran to the road crying for her son.

Jacob was still alive when she reached him. She threw herself on the ground beside him and cradled his head in her arms. She kissed his forehead and ran her fingers through his wavy hair.

"They have killed me, Ma ...I made a big mistake with my life... I should have listened to you ..."

"Don't say a word, son. Please don't go. You are all I have. I am the one who betrayed you. Forgive me, God," she whimpered.

As the warm blood soaked the earth and stained both their clothes, Jacob felt faint. He knew the end was near.

"Forgive me, Ma. I did wrong ... I am paying the price ..." It was becoming more difficult to speak. "Put your ear close, Ma ... there is something I want to tell you ... under the banana trees, there is another box ... three hundred thousand katas ... send Edwin outside the province ... if he stays here he will fall into the same trap ... Ma, I am feeling thirsty ... give me some water ..."

Jacob's chest heaved twice for air and then his body lay still.

When Philipson arrived in his brand new imported SUV minutes later, after getting a call from Kamat, Ben the driver had to pry Ma's hands from Jacob's lifeless body.

She wept uncontrollably as she was raised to her feet. But the moment she saw Philipson she stopped crying. She looked him straight in the eye and said, "You killed my son."

The police arrived and took Jacob's body away to the government hospital.

Ma walked back home. Elsie saw her bloodstained clothes she began wailing.

"We both have to cry and our crying will never end. They killed both our children. Rosie and Jacob are both dead."

The two women clung to each other as they cried.

The Sub-Divisional Officer of Police picked up the bloodstained copy of Ché's Guerilla Warfare and surmised that Jacob might be the missing piece of the puzzle. But the puzzle got infinitely more complicated within the next half hour.

*\*\*\**

Philipson was satisfied. He had eliminated the threat. He had trusted Jacob and had great hopes for him but Jacob would not fit in with his new plans. Chief Minister Chapang would be pleased with the liquidation and would think of him as being decisive and ruthless. Kamat would be thrilled with the money and the action.

"Sau Ben, let us go home," said Philipson.

"Who killed Sau Jacob, Sau Philipson?" asked Ben. "He was such a nice guy."

"I don't know, Sau Ben. He may have had some secret quarrel. These days you never know."

On reaching the house Ben honked the horn twice for the gate to be opened.

There was a tap on the window of the SUV on the passenger's side. Philipson rolled down the tinted window to see who it was.

The automatic spoke once, the bullet hitting him between the eyes and exiting through the far corner of the rear windscreen.

Before a stunned Ben or the guards could react, Major Kapwanga jumped into the idling jeep and sped away in a swirl of dust, wheels screaming.

***

"We have to stop weeping. We must save Edwin from the same fate," said Ma.

"I have nothing to live for. My Rosie is dead," wept Nau Elsie.

"Let us change our clothes. I have some work to do in the garden."

She found the tin box with the money. Hiding it under her apron she rushed back to the house and showed it to Rosie's mother.

"This is the money Jacob left for both of us. We must send Edwin outside our province to Ultapur to study. That was Jacob's last wish. You stay in the house and guard this money for me while I go and look for Edwin."

Then she ran as fast as her feeble legs would carry her. With her apron flying in the wind and her frail arms flailing, she ran towards the playing field of Edwin's school.

The author welcomes comments at:
aa-books@outlook.com

For more information about the author's books:
www.abiealexander.com